I0822528

Donovan was tall. His hair blew about his shoulders, and his long, dark jacket hung open. If someone had seen him, just in that instant, he might have resembled a gunslinger. His hand was poised near his hip, and he turned, giving the old dead musician the smallest physical target possible.

"Show's over, Johnny," he said. "It's time to go back to sleep."

"Step aside, witch," Johnny hissed. "This ain't your fight. These are Johnny's streets; got to take care of business, and got no beef with you."

"I'm afraid that's not true," Donovan said. He'd been working something slowly out of his pocket, and he held it up. He glanced right, and left. Where he stood, the alley ended. It was bisected by another, older and smaller path, barely a walkway down the side of the club to the street. "Those beyond you are my friends. They are not yours to take. This is not your night."

"You can't stop it," Johnny said, fingers still dancing on the strings. "You and your pet crow are too late to the show. The song is nearly sung."

Donovan didn't answer. He twisted his wrist, and the item in his hand, the small pouch that Bullfinch had given him, flicked open. Dust spun into the air and dropped at his feet, and Donovan began to speak. He spoke low and fast, and the dust spread—right, left, ahead and behind. It glittered like dark diamonds, and then, as the chant continued, it began to glow.

Donovan glanced up and caught Johnny's gaze a final time. The dead man's fingers never faltered, but some of the cockiness had left his stance. The glittering, glowing trail of dust slid toward him, gaining speed.

"Ashes to ashes," Donovan said softly. "Dust to dust. I stand at the crossroads, Blind Johnny Jones. I stand at the crossroads, and I'm calling you home."

I would like to thank, first and foremost, the love of my life, Patricia Lee Macomber, and my wonderful children, Stephanie, Bill, Zach, Zane, and Katie, who put up with my enthusiastic outbursts about the world of Donovan DeChance on a regular basis, and who have always loved and supported me. I'd like to thank Kurt Criscione, the keeper of the series bible for this and other works of mine, all of which seem to constantly intertwine, David Dodd, for helping me turn Crossroad Press into something more than a hobby, and Aaron Rosenberg, for not only handling most of our print books—but for teaching me how to do it myself. Last but not least, I'd like to thank the words, and the magic, for being my companions in life.

Mystique Press is an imprint of Crossroad Press.

Cover illustration by Bob Eggleton
Design by Aaron Rosenberg
ISBN 978-1-949914-36-8 — ISBN 978-1-949914-37-5 (pbk.)

For information address Crossroad Press at 141 Brayden Dr., Hertford, NC 27944
www.crossroadpress.com

First Crossroad Press Edition

THE DeCHANCE CHRONICLES
VOLUME FOUR

KALI'S TALE

DAVID NIALL WILSON

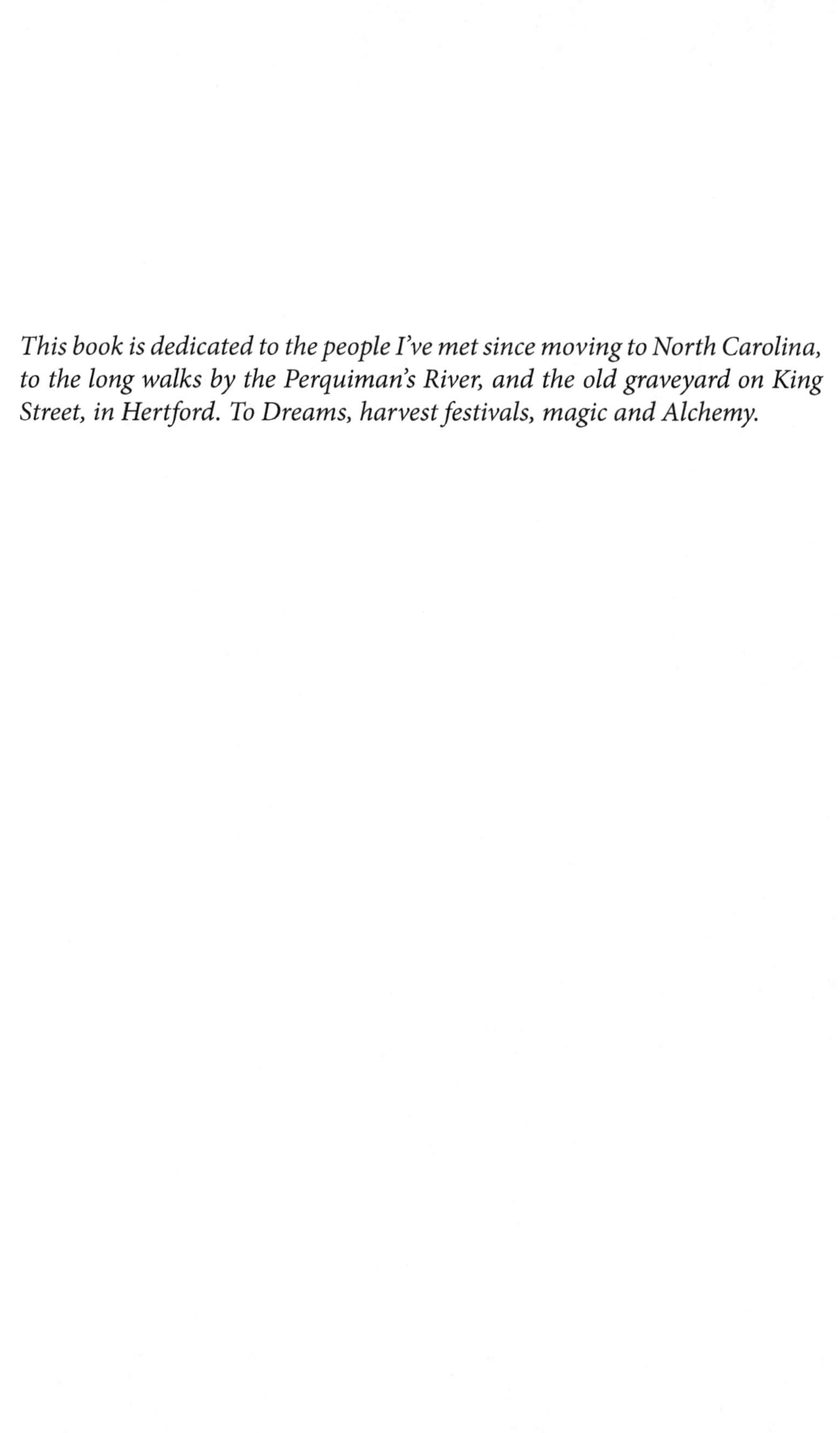

This book is dedicated to the people I've met since moving to North Carolina, to the long walks by the Perquiman's River, and the old graveyard on King Street, in Hertford. To Dreams, harvest festivals, magic and Alchemy.

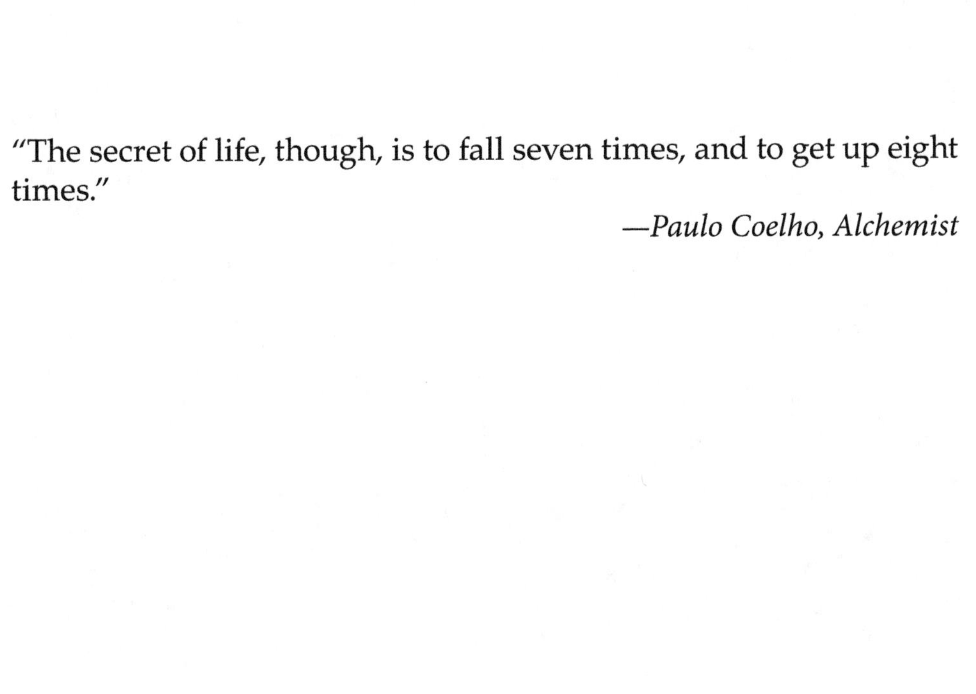

"The secret of life, though, is to fall seven times, and to get up eight times."

—Paulo Coelho, Alchemist

AUTHOR'S NOTE

This will mark the fourth book in *The DeChance Chronicles*, which starts with the novel *Heart of a Dragon,* moves on to *Vintage Soul* (which was actually written first—long story for another time) and the novella *My Soul to Keep* which is the origin story for Donovan DeChance, and not to be missed by fans of the series.

This book also accomplishes something I have intended for some time. In this volume, *The DeChance Chronicles* make a direct connection and crossover to another series I write, O.C.L.T. In that series, I've written the novel *The Parting* and the novella *The Temple of Camazotz*. The characters Rebecca York and Geoffrey Bullfinch appear in this novel, as does Cletus J. Diggs, from my book *The Not Quite Right Reverend Cletus J. Diggs & The Currently Accepted Habits of Nature*. This book takes place largely in Old Mill, North Carolina, which is Cletus' stomping grounds. My books and my stories have long shared certain locations—San Valencez, Lavender, and Friendly California, Old Mill, North Carolina, and Random Illinois. If you enjoy this book, you should look up the titles above—you'll find some old friends waiting.

If the story *The Preacher's Marsh*, which involves a legend mentioned in this book, appeals to you, that novella is also available. In North Carolina I've found that all roads lead to Highway 17, and in my writing, it seems the same may be true.

There will, with the grace of whatever power watches over me, be many more Donovan DeChance books in the future, and many more adventures for Cletus J. Diggs and for the agents of O.C. L.T. I hope you'll join me. I'm always ready to tell a story.

David Niall Wilson
Just off to the side of The Great Dismal Swamp

CHAPTER ONE

The sun had set over the skyline of San Valencez an hour earlier. Relaxing in the one leather armchair not covered in a layer of books, manuscripts, and scrolls, Donovan DeChance had dimmed the lights in most of his home, leaving the fireplace flickering merrily. Cleo, his Egyptian Mau, lay curled on the arm of the couch, her tail flipping absently over the leather cover of a seventeenth century treatise on alchemy. At the top of the ornate mantle, the old crow Asmodeus watched over the entire scene placidly. It was as close to relaxation as Donovan had felt in years, and so, he didn't trust it.

When the lamp on his table emitted a soft purple glow, he was almost relieved. The lamp was one of his most cherished possessions, a bonus payment for services rendered many years in the past. It was a very old piece, handmade and beautiful. The base was the trunk of a bronze tree with ten arms. From each of those arms dangled an ancient coin. There was a heavy rod running up the center and this was topped with a spiked finial that connected the slag-glass shade to the base.

The shade had twenty-two slats, running through a subtle range of violets and purples. The end of each was embossed with a single letter from the Hebrew alphabet. As was true of most of the furnishings in his home, the lamp was more than it seemed. When someone approached his door, or tried in some other way to breach the defenses and wards he'd set, it illuminated. The brighter the light, the more imminent the danger. The light this evening was deep and pure. He didn't know who was approaching, but they were not approaching in anger, and—as he was familiar with how the lamp reacted to those he was closest to—its warning was doubly interesting. There was something else, as well, something more subtle and less familiar, but not threatening.

"So, Cleo," Donovan said. "Shall I meet our guest, or wait for them to announce their arrival?"

Cleo glanced up and gave a soft meow, then laid her head back on her front paws and watched him. The cat, also his familiar, was another warning system that never failed him. He glanced up at Asmodeus, who glared back at him balefully. No reaction.

With a shrug, he set aside the scroll he'd been translating, balancing it precariously atop a pile of large tomes filled with images, plates, and hieroglyphics from an ancient temple. He was preparing to scan them into his archive, and so they'd worked their way to the top of the pile. Then, seeing that they were broad, stacked carefully, and sturdy, he'd begun using them as another horizontal workspace, and the scanning had been shelved, for the moment. A lot of other things needed to be shelved as well. He glanced around, shook his head, and turned toward the door.

The warning system also gave him the opportunity to unbind the wards on the door. He did so slowly, letting his senses seep out through the cracks and up through the vents. His home had been invaded exactly once, and he had no intention of letting it happen again—particularly not when he knew someone was coming. He felt nothing dangerous. In fact, the tug that he felt warmed his veins slightly, and brought a flush to his cheeks. He rested his hand on the doorframe, just for a second, getting his senses under control.

"Vanessa," he said, as he opened the door. "This is truly an unexpected pleasure."

She stood in the hallway, watching him. She was nearly as tall as he with long, golden blonde hair. She was slender and shapely with the grace and beauty of a supermodel, and that was only the beginning of her allure. When she smiled, he caught just the hint of a glimmer from the perfect ivory of her fangs. He also felt her blood. He felt it actually pressing out against the inside of his veins and arteries, felt a subtle shift in the rhythm of his heart.

It was the first time he'd stood in her presence since saving her from becoming the final and most important ingredient in a wizard's bid for immortality. As a show of gratitude, she'd shared a few drops of her blood, in a small bottle of cognac, with Donovan and his lover, Amethyst.

"Are you going to invite me in, Donovan?" she asked. "I've never been here before. Some of the old curses die slowly."

Donovan stepped back, smiled, and waved her in with a gallant flourish. She crossed the threshold like an orchid-scented breeze. She brushed against him as she entered, the silk of her dress tickling his arm. He caught the curl of her smile and took a very deep breath.

"Where is Preston?" he asked, closing the door behind her. "I haven't spoken to him in some time. I was thinking just the other day that I owed you a visit. I trust you've recovered from your—trial?"

"I'm as good as I've ever been," she replied. "Better, probably, because such an experience tends to brighten the taste of the world, don't you think? If you grow too complacent, you take gifts for granted."

"I am sure that a lot of lessons were learned," Donovan replied. "Security has tightened all over the city, I'm told. I've taken some new precautions, and I'd hate to be the one trying to break in and take another thing that belonged to Amethyst. She's looking for someone, or something, to take out the frustration of being fooled the first time on."

"Going to offer a girl a drink?" Vanessa asked. She glanced down coyly, and Donovan flushed. He hurried to the bar, keeping his face averted and trying not to show how she attracted him. It wasn't simply a natural attraction, it was part of her power—a glamour that was stronger with her than with any undead he'd ever encountered. It was amplified still more by their shared blood bond.

She stepped up behind him so quickly that her scent stole his breath. She reached around him, took the goblet of wine he'd poured before he could spill the rich, red liquid over the edge and onto his hand, and then pulled back with a bright, vibrant laugh.

"I'm sorry," she said. "It's my nature to tease, and you certainly deserve more of me. I feel it too, you know? The blood? Ours is a strange bond. I have never blood bonded with a living man or woman. It's unique. It excites me. It gives me a new perspective. Did you know I can share your senses, just a bit? That I can see things through you, and through Amethyst, that I can only dream of in my private darkness. I owe you my second life, and it is not a debt I will forget."

Just for a second, Donovan wondered if the reverse would ever be true. What would it be like to sense that hunger? To feel that power? Taking a deep, relieved breath, he poured a second glass of wine, and turned to face her.

"So," he said. "As much as I'd like to believe it's my captivating personality that drew you here, I suspect there is more to this visit. Is there trouble with the Council? Is Johndrow alright? Vein?"

"You are right to assume this isn't a casual visit," she said, "but not to believe that you will only see me when I have a need. You have lived a long life, and yet, I have lived one twice as long, and I suspect we both have a number of years left to walk parallel trails. Someday you are going to need something that I can provide, and when that time comes…"

"You don't need to say it," Donovan said. "I know."

She nodded and sipped her wine.

"I'm here about Kali," she said at last. "You remember, the young one that Vein has bonded with?"

"They were not fully bonded when I last saw them," Donovan replied, "but I suspected it was a matter of time. He was very protective."

"As he was of me," she said. "It's his nature. It's an odd tendency for one of my kind, but endearing. Vein tells me things he would tell no one else, because…"

"Of the blood bond," Donovan finished. "I believe that someday soon we must sit down and record this. The variations and connections that are possible, the benefits, and the downside. I have a great number of volumes of undead lore, but the literature on the blood bond is skimpy. It is also oddly void of *any* mention of humans and vampires bonding without compulsion."

"The lore is rare because the bond is intimate," she said. She smiled, and he had to fight to keep a tremble from his hand.

"Kali is going to come before the Council in a few days' time," Vanessa said. "She is going to ask for the Council's support in a blood quest. She has fought her rage and hatred for a very long time, and now it clouds her judgment. She will seek the one who made her, and she will either destroy him or be destroyed. You know of this practice?"

"I do," Donovan said. "If I'm not mistaken, Johndrow himself completed the blood quest. A very long time ago."

Vanessa nodded. "There are a number of ways to come to the blood. We are very careful in these times to turn few, if any. Those we do, we've come to love, or to trust, and truly wish to become part of our culture. We have the Council, and we have laws. There was even a time when we enforced them."

"Kali's was not a pleasant becoming," Donovan said. "She hinted at that, when last I saw her, but it was more an anger simmering below the surface, something she drew strength from."

"It was a horror," Vanessa said. "That is how she describes it. I must confess…things have changed a great deal since I was turned. I was taken without consent, but I grew to love the blood—to cherish the gift of my beauty unfaded over decades and centuries. I was taken from circumstances that were not good, and made into a princess of the night. Kali was taken from a happy home. She did not even know of our kind until she was dragged into the fold. She was kept prisoner and servant for many, many unpleasant years. I wish that I thought the Council would help her, but I am nearly certain they will not."

"What of the laws?" Donovan asked.

"They are weak old men," she said. "Johndrow would go—and he would fight. I would certainly go; I am bonded, but we are bound by the manacles of our own more civilized existence. If we don't agree, we don't act. We don't put the others in danger by going off on our own, and they will not want this quest."

"She will be forbidden?"

"Would you like to try forbidding one such as Kali?" Vanessa laughed. "It is her choice. It will be Vein's choice, and that of his companions. They will follow her, but none of them is very old, or powerful, and Vein lacks control. He has not been far from my side since I turned him, and he has no idea how to protect himself, or how to remain in the shadows. He will see it as new freedom, and I fear his recklessness will get them all in trouble."

"What can I do?" Donovan asked. "I don't believe they are going to accept me as a traveling partner or chaperone. I assume you have a plan?"

She nodded again. "I believe so. I have a pretty good idea where they are headed. I know they are going to need a more powerful bloodstone, and I intend to visit Amethyst and purchase it for them. I'll send them around to her later, but I'm not going to mention you…I'm hoping you'll sort of tag along in the shadows. Maybe even get there ahead of them."

"Oh?" Donovan asked.

"Oh yes," she chuckled softly. "How do you feel about The Great Dismal Swamp?"

CHAPTER TWO

When Vanessa had gone, Donovan reset his wards and walked to his desk. He took his wine glass with him, and the bottle. It was looking like a long night's research lay ahead of him, and he was going to have to get some help. It had been a long time since he'd visited the Carolinas, and he never went on a mission cold. It was an old place, and very powerful, and it was one of the earliest settled areas in the United States.

Donovan knew that the land he'd walked for so long held powers and secrets that predated the concerns of modern men. Even the oldest of the dark underworld of San Valencez were young compared to some of the men, women, and creatures who walked the Earth, and if you intended to walk into the den of such a being, you needed to have your facts in order.

The mention of The Great Dismal Swamp had piqued his interest. He'd heard some interesting tales coming out of that area recently. He'd heard rumors of meddling with ancient Gods and fertility rites. There were other tales, darker ones, of creatures deep in the swamp, still hidden from civilization and light, drawing in on themselves and angry with the invasion of the daylight world.

He had his own memories of the area, but they were old, and he hadn't visited in generations. Most of the places he'd frequented in those times no longer existed and most of the people he'd known were long gone.

Donovan had books that detailed powers and mages. He could trace most of their journeys through early America chronicle their accomplishments and adventures, and most importantly insure that others learned from their mistakes. The problem with such a huge repository of information was in knowing how to use it. The computers helped. He had scanned, indexed, backed up and saved more occult data than, as a young man, he could have conceived to exist. He'd perused most of it, studied much of it, and cataloged all that he'd encountered, but it was still like looking for the proverbial needle in a haystack to extract specific data when it was needed—albeit a very familiar haystack. In times like this, he preferred to consult subject matter experts. He'd earned favors from a lot of people over the years, and he thought it was time to call one of them in.

He sat at his desk and picked up the phone. He didn't need to look up the number or any number. He smiled. As Amethyst liked to joke, he could take an old rotary dial phone and one-up the cell phones that have an "app" for that every time. He had a charm for it. He pressed the buttons on the old phone in an intricate pattern and whispered a name.

"Bullfinch."

A moment later, the phone began to ring, and Donovan sat back, thinking about his old friend, and wondering where the call would find him.

"Bullfinch." The bright, cheerful voice widened Donovan's smile.

"It's Donovan, Geoffrey," he said. "It's been too long."

"That it has," Bullfinch replied. "I must say, you are the last person I'd expected to hear from just now. There are big changes afoot. We must talk about them, and soon."

"I've heard rumors," Donovan said. "It's interesting. This organization of yours has promise. As long as they respect the balance."

"That is the hope," Bullfinch chuckled. "That has always been the hope. What can I do for you, Donovan? I'm guessing you didn't call just to chat, as much as I'd enjoy that."

"I'm researching a little vacation," Donovan said. "A working vacation. I'm familiar with the general area, The Great Dismal Swamp. What's bothering me is the particular location. It's a town called Old Mill, and if my calculations are correct, it's an intersection of a greater ley line with a sort of gridline of lesser conduits. Also, I've heard or read something about the area. Since it's close to your recent home ground, and swamp magic falls more in your bailiwick than my own, I thought of you. I'm sure I have the information I need here somewhere, but where to look?"

"You have my interest," Bullfinch said. "We've been keeping close tabs on that area for some time now. There has been more than a usual amount of activity in the area. I know of one woman, Nettie, who practices the arts, but she's a recluse. You can get her to talk if you take whiskey, but her answers almost always come at a price. What exactly are you after?"

"I don't have all the details," Donovan said, "but I do know that the one we are going in after is undead. From the look and feel of it, very old, and very powerful. There is something I'm not remembering about this-- something more. I haven't heard any particular reports of vampire activity in that area, and yet, I've heard something, at some point, that I can't quite recall."

There was silence on the other end of the line, and for a moment Donovan thought the connection had been broken. Then Bullfinch replied.

"Old boy, you are walking into the wolf's den," he said. "How soon do you have to do this?"

"I'm not sure, exactly," Donovan said. "I'll be chaperoning a group of young undead who don't know I'm tagging along. It's a long story. My guess is that the High Council is not going to offer full support—it's a blood quest. If that's the case, they'll have to drive. It's a long way from San Valencez to North Carolina. I think I have several days, maybe a week. Why?"

"I think this one is going to require face to face," Bullfinch said. "I don't mean to be enigmatic, but this is not your average case, Donovan. If the one you seek is who I suspect it might be, it means he is active again, or has been recently, and we were not aware. There are a lot of strange things going on in that area, but as you say, none of them have involved the undead. I want a few days to gather information. There must be missing person's reports. There have likely been sightings, and if your young vampire was created there, there will be records of that family."

"I know her only as Kali," Donovan said. "I suspect she took the name of the Destroyer upon herself. She is not old in the blood, but she is strong willed. The fact that she is here and not serving the one who created her in the depths of the swamp speaks volumes. In fact, it makes no sense to me at all."

"She may have found a way to hurt him," Bullfinch said. "It's the only way she could have gotten beyond his influence without being called back, or destroyed herself. You may want to find out what it was she did. It's unlikely your target will fall for the same sort of attack twice, but it might give you a starting place."

"Where are you?" Donovan asked.

"As it turns out, I'm not far from Old Mill. I'm in the mountains near Asheville. There has been some nasty business here with dead who don't seem inclined to accept their lot in life—or their lack of the same. I have been busy quieting spirits, and visiting an old friend. You remember Rebecca York?"

Donovan smiled again. "I hope you'll give her my regards," Donovan said. "Also, you can tell her that the item she sent to me is safe, and unlikely to see the light of day, or to get close to any water, anytime soon."

"I will do that. I'm sure it will bring a smile."

"So," Donovan said, "I will come to you, then, before I continue on. Amethyst can keep an eye on our young friends and try to keep them out of trouble while I'm gone. She will be joining us. Another tale for firelight and wine, but suffice it to say that she and I share somewhat of a blood bond with one of those on the quest. It's more personal than usual."

"A blood bond with a human is a story worth more than wine," Bullfinch said. "Give me a few days. Also, you might want to search your archive for references to early North American Alchemy. I think you may find a few things that will be of interest, and it might prepare you for what I have to tell you and show you."

"Alchemy," Donovan repeated. "I have not thought of alchemy in a very long time. I studied that art, you know? In fact, I had an old volume on the subject in front of me just this week."

"I do," Bullfinch said. "All of us search, from time to time, for our personal Philosopher's Stone. Not all of those who practiced alchemy were after spiritual truth, or growth, however. Like any other human endeavor, eventually the questions of power and gain intruded."

"Thank you," Donovan said. "I will do as you say, and I will make my preparations. If nothing else, knowing that we may be up against more than just a vampire old and powerful enough to steal our souls is a good thing, I suppose, though—and not for the first time—it makes me question my own sanity."

Bullfinch laughed.

"If sanity were a prerequisite for the lives we lead," he said, "we'd both have chosen different fields."

"I suppose you're right. And when this is all over, you need to make a visit to San Valencez. There is the matter of a book you have been promising to autograph for me for a very long time."

"Consider it a 'date'. Now, I'm afraid I need to get back out to a certain graveyard before the moon gets much higher. Take care, Donovan, and I will see you soon."

The line went dead, and Donovan leaned back in the chair. Cleo leaped up into his lap, and he curled her into his arm, stroking absently behind her ears.

"Alchemy, vampires, blood quests," he said with a sigh. "Why is it, Cleo, that every time someone comes to me with a simple problem it turns into something…more?"

She glanced up at him and let out a long, chiding meow. He ruffled her head with a laugh and sat up. He tapped the login sequence into his keyboard, and then whispered the charm that completed the code. His screen illuminated, and he set to work. It was shaping up to be a long, sleepless night.

CHAPTER THREE

The Council of Elders met in Johndrow's penthouse. Despite recent trouble, his security was among the best available, and his flair for entertaining was unmatched. Since his lover, Vanessa, had been returned to him, he had seldom been seen beyond the confines of his own walls. Security had been tightened. In addition to the gnomish guardians traditionally employed by the Council, Johndrow had added his own staff. They were dark, slender, and very dangerous, and their services had not come cheaply. Money wasn't an object—security was.

Besides, the occasion of this gathering was of a more personal nature. One of the young ones, a girl named Kali, wished to address her elders and receive their blessing. She was unlikely to get it, Johndrow knew, but the old ways still held sway, and certain matters required their attention, even when the outcome was already known.

In this case, it would be a request for support in a blood quest. Vampirism wore the twin badges of gift and curse. Some came to it gracefully, willingly, and without regret. Others were dragged in screaming and clawing for the life that would be forever denied them. Almost all who came to the blood grew to be pleased with the powers and benefits of their new existence. This did nothing to ease the anger of those who had never been given a choice. If that anger and bitterness could not be overcome, there was only one course open. Seek out the one who made you and destroy them—or reach final death in the attempt. To ignore such a call led to madness, and there was no shortage of the insane among the ranks of the undead.

Johndrow himself had tracked and destroyed his maker. It was something he rarely spoke of and even more rarely dwelled upon. It was too easy to return to the anger, and to feel that even final death did not erase such a debt. He understood Kali's rage only too well, but it would not matter.

Most of the members of the Council were content. They had been seduced, brought to the blood slowly and with, if not love, at least respect. They did not feel or understand the rage, and they would not condone it in others. Blood quests drew attention to the darkness. They were messy, dangerous, and too often ended with the young ones either enslaved to a much more powerful sire, or destroyed utterly. Conflicts between powerful undead were avoided at all costs; sending this girl on a quest to kill one of their own would seem like an act of aggression on their part, and the sad fact was, Johndrow knew, that they'd grown too timid to face the thought of their scripted little lives being disrupted.

He would vote for the blood quest. Vanessa would, as well, and Joel. Probably Ligaya. That left too many opposed. The Resendez brothers were just back in town, and unlikely to vote on anything that might disrupt their efforts to get their own house in order. Lydia and her Adriana would oppose the quest because they would not understand it. Nystrom and Grimshaw would claim it was bad for business. Andrew Corwyn was a wild card, because he would normally side with his own lover, Meredith, who was not present. Corwyn still wore spectacles; an affectation carried over from his human life that he believed made him look more intelligent. He was not a violent type, and without Meredith's wiser mind involved, there was just no predicting what he might say or do. Copper and Alicia Contreaux were still down in Louisiana, which was a shame. While Copper had come willingly enough to the darkness, Alicia had not, and both of them had first-hand knowledge of the worst of their kind. Sometimes they seemed less like a council and more like a nest full of bickering old hens.

He stood and watched as they entered, greeting each in turn. Vanessa flitted up and down the main hall like an elegant butterfly, her heels impossibly tall, her skirt enticingly short, and her grace intoxicating. She captivated them, one by one, and in doing so gave Johndrow the leisure to gauge their mood. He suspected they had all come ready to enjoy his hospitality, but with their minds firmly set. As Lydia and Adriana slipped through the door last, late as always and awash in apologies and dark, exotic perfumes, Johndrow fell in behind them. In his wake, a dark form melted from the shadows, and then a second. They stepped up to either side of the elevator and pressed their palms tightly to the wall. Turning to face one another, they spoke very softly. Johndrow could not hear their words, but he felt them. They crawled over his skin and vibrated through the air. He did not look back, but he knew that, had he done so, he'd have seen nothing but a smooth wall where the elevator should have been.

Briefly, he wondered where the elevator had gone, and who would see it on the other side.

In the den, the others had taken up stations. Joel and Ligaya stood with Vanessa near the bar. Lydia and Adriana were draped across a large leather chair and one another, tattooed limbs entwined to create one large, spider-like creature. Lydia was an artist. She'd been drawing and painting for centuries, but had recently taken up the art of the tattoo and other forms of body modification. Adriana was her muse, her inspiration, and from time to time, her drawing and cutting board. Prior to his bonding with Vanessa, Johndrow had spent some time with the two. He smiled at them and nodded. Now it was the Resendez brothers, their dark, wavy hair and even darker eyes, who attended the pair. Johndrow wished them luck.

Nystrom, Grimshaw, and Corwyn stood a bit detached from the others. They leaned in close, as if discussing world-shattering secrets. Johndrow suspected that they were drooling over what vintage he might provide for the refreshments. Johndrow walked over to join Vanessa, Joel, and Ligaya.

"When do you expect the young ones?" Joel asked.

"Not for a while yet," Johndrow said. "I figured I'd break out a bottle and soften up the crowd for her. It's going to be rough enough if they're in a good mood."

Ligaya scanned the room and shook her head.

"They will not condone it," she said. "If we could get some of the others, perhaps, we could sway them, but without Copper and Alicia, and with Meredith not here to control Andrew, I'm afraid…"

"I know," Johndrow said wearily. "It is a formality at best. It is also given that, regardless of what we say, they will go. You know that, and I know that, and everyone in this room knows it as well. They are not thinking of the well-being of one of the young…they are already trying to figure out how to distance themselves from the outcome should anything go wrong."

"You can bet they'll come back by to congratulate her if she succeeds," Vanessa said. She frowned.

Johndrow studied his lover's face. She had a deeper connection to these proceedings than any of the others. She had brought Vein to the blood, and

Vein was Kali's companion. If Kali went, Vein would follow, and if Vein went, his 'posse' of young vampires would follow in his wake like so much shadow and dust. The potential for disaster was great and the likelihood of success small. It was a fool's errand under the best of circumstances, and in the company of a group of young hotheads who thought they owned the night it was downright foolish.

"I would go myself," Johndrow said, "if I thought she'd let me. I might not succeed—I have no blood hatred for her sire, and I know very little of him. He may be truly ancient, or he may be only slightly older than she is. I have no way to know."

"There is a way," Joel said softly.

They all turned to him. He met their gaze levelly. "You know there is," he said. "If she would allow it, we could all know. Perhaps that knowledge would make our decision an easier one. If the one she seeks is not so old, or so powerful, then there may be less harm in it than we fear. In any case, if the Council's worries center on our secrets being open to the day walkers, then getting Vein and his friends out of the city for a little vacation is in our interests. He is not...patient."

They all chuckled at this.

Johndrow walked to the bar and pressed an inset button beneath the counter. Above them, doors slid to either side, and beyond those boards an amazing array of bottles and decanters were stored, some laying down to breathe while others—the whiskeys and cognacs—stood stoppered and ready. The drinks were Johndrow's passion. He had collected them over the centuries, adding drops of the blood of famous men and women, great artists, royalty, musicians and politicians. When the bar was fully open, he turned to Joel.

"What will it be tonight, old friend? Passion? Romance? Diplomacy? Genius?"

"If you asked me any other time," Joel replied, "I'd have said that the Council needed all the diplomacy it could muster. Tonight? What have you got in the way of adventure? What have you got to build a flame in the heart?"

Johndrow laughed. "I think it will take more than a good drink to do that for this crowd," he said.

There was a blue-tinted bottle on the second shelf, and he leaned in to retrieve it. It was more than a liter—an odd size and shape—and as Johndrow turned and displayed it, the room fell silent. They might have disagreed on a lot of things, but on one point they were solid. The magic that came out of Johndrow's collection was not to be missed, and as often as not, it really was magic.

"Ladies, Gentlemen," he began. "The time has come to dispense with the pleasantries, and to begin preparing ourselves for the issue at hand. Before we do that, though, I have a story for you—and a gift."

An appreciative murmur circled the room, and Johndrow's smile widened. "Bear with me," he said. "It's an exquisite vintage, but, without the story it is less than it might be, and to drink it beneath its potential would be wasteful indeed."

Before he could continue, there was a commotion in the hall. Johndrow turned, irritated. One of the dark, slender security men stood in the doorway, waiting stoically. Johndrow believed the man would have stood there through the entire meeting, waiting patiently to deliver his message. It was their way.

"Yes?" he said.

"Your other guests have arrived." The man's voice whispered like released gas into the room. It was a sing-song whistle, and he clapped it off as quickly as he released it, leaving his words to echo strangely in the heavy air.

Johndrow hesitated. He hated to be interrupted, and he hated it even more when he was about to serve one of his delicacies, but in this instance his intention was to support Kali's request. It would not do for him to show his ire where the others might misinterpret it.

"Show them in," he said, nodding to the security guard.

A moment later, Kali stepped into the room. She was a beautiful girl, taken at the age of eighteen, with long, long legs and dark, silky hair and unreadable black eyes. She was flanked by Vein, Bones, Pierce, Shade, and Bruno—the oddball of their group. Bruno was the youngest of them all in the blood, but he'd been turned when he was forty. He towered over the others, and looked more like one of their fathers, or a bodyguard, than a companion. Most vampires were created when young and beautiful. Not all, of course. Joel and Grimshaw, for instance, had been turned later in life, and Johndrow himself had been in his thirties.

The others were thin, dark, and affected every modern vampiric stereotype possible. They wore dark leather, dark glasses, too much jewelry, clothing that looked like something that belonged on the stage of a rock concert, and they collected followers like band groupies. This, of course, rather than making them stand out in the world of day walkers, only made them 'popular' in the eyes of the city's youth, a nuisance to local law enforcement, and thus basically invisible to the world.

Kali stepped forward. Her dark eyes flashed, and the anger seething just beneath the surface of her pale skin gave her a dangerous, electric aspect.

"So," she said. "This is how it works. You dress up, you gather in the shadows to have a drink and decide—what? My life? My future?"

"Your life and your future, so long as you don't endanger those of the rest of us, are your own," Johndrow replied. "This meeting is to decide whether we will sanction or support you."

Vein stepped up beside Kali. Though his eyes flashed defiance, there was a slight tremble in his voice when he spoke.

"Whatever is decided here," he said, "she has our support. Mine," he turned and nodded toward his companions, "and theirs."

"That won't be worth spit in the wind if you encounter an ancient," Juan Resendez said, stepping forward. "You, them, a dozen more like you, will be as inconsequential as mosquitoes to a meat sack."

Vein wanted to say something. He wanted to snap back and pose, but somehow he bit it back, and Johndrow almost smiled. The boy had changed. Ever since nearly losing his life in a failed attempt to save Vanessa, he'd shown signs that he might actually mature. That he might survive.

"He's right, you know," Johndrow said, drawing all their attention back to himself. He made a decision in that instant and turned, placing the blue bottle back into its slot over the bar. "For another time," he said. Instead, he grabbed a bottle of cognac from the lowest shelf.

He turned back to face Kali. A plan was forming—something Joel had said. He didn't think it would turn the tide, but it might level the playing field a bit.

"I am going to make a request, and a suggestion," Johndrow said.

Kali started to step forward again, and to speak, but Johndrow held up a hand, and Vein grabbed her shoulders to steady her.

"There is a way we can know," Johndrow said. "You are not blood bonded to any of us. Perhaps you and Vein are joined—but now? You might as well come from the blood of another universe. We do not know the name of your sire—nor do you. We don't know his age, or his location. For all we know he could be one of the first. If that were true, as impossible as it might sound, we would all be, as my friend Juan so aptly put it, no more than annoying mosquitoes. I propose a sharing. Your blood, your life, to ours. I propose that you let us see, and from that seeing know what you face. Do you know what it is that I ask?"

"Are you crazy?" Nystrom said softly. "You would ask us to…"

"What is it, old man?" Vein's head swiveled like that of a dangerous snake. His voice and eyes were flat and cold. "You don't consider her blood a substitute for that of some fallen poet or dead king? You're disappointed?"

"That's enough," Johndrow said. "We are well aware the intimacy, and honor," he bowed slightly toward Kali, "that this would entail. It also involves a great deal of trust on your part. But, if you agree…"

"You will know," Kali said. Her voice was measured, controlled but filled with tension.

"We will," Johndrow agreed. "Combined with our own memories, our own knowledge, it could reveal the totality of your quest."

"And it could shut it down," Vanessa said. She laid a hand on Johndrow's arm. "You realize this, too?"

Kali looked from one to the other. Then she scanned the rest of the elders, spending a moment studying each of their faces. No one in the room moved.

"They share too," she said, nodding toward Vein, and then their other companions. "If I share with you—with those I barely know—I will share with my family. This is allowed?"

Johndrow nodded. "Of course."

Kali stepped forward. She held out her arm, palm up. She met Johndrow's gaze and held it. He stepped forward to meet her. Vanessa went to the bar and returned with a crystal tumbler. Johndrow drew a nail lightly over the vein in Kali's wrist. He stroked back and forth, as if mesmerized by it—lost in what was to come. Vanessa pressed herself around him, insinuated her arms beneath his, and held the glass beneath Kali's arm. With a swift slice of his nail, Johndrow opened Kali's vein. Blood seeped, and Vanessa moved quickly to capture it. Almost the second her skin parted, it began to heal. Blood flowed for only a matter of seconds, but it was enough. Several large drops fell into the goblet, and when the flow stopped, Vanessa unwound herself and returned to the bar. Johndrow held Kali's arm a moment longer and then, almost reluctantly, he released her and pulled back. He brought his finger up, as if to lick it clean, then thought better of it, controlled himself and joined Vanessa.

He rinsed his hands, dried them, and unstopped the bottle of cognac.

He poured two fingers into the tumbler containing Kali's blood and swirled it slowly. Vanessa pulled a small silver funnel from a drawer and placed it in the neck of the bottle. Johndrow poured the liquor back into the bottle and Vanessa replaced the stopper. She took the bottle then, flipped it, and flipped it again. She spun it in her hands, so fast the label—a very old label—blurred and then came back into focus. She placed the bottle on the bar. Johndrow took down a silver tray, and then lined it with tumblers similar to the one that had held the blood.

Very slowly and carefully, he poured. There was plenty left in the bottle when he was finished, and he stoppered it carefully. He left the bottle on the bar, and turned with the tray in his hand.

"It is yours to do," he said to Kali. "It is yours to share."

She nodded and took the tray. Vein stepped back and stood with his companions. He watched Kali with such concentration and intensity that Johndrow doubted he was aware of the room or the elders at all. For Vein, even more than the others, this would be a special moment. He and Kali already had a growing bond. This would cement and seal it.

Kali circled the room then, carefully, almost deferentially, she knelt before each of them, and offered the tray. Each of them took their glass in silence. She lingered before Vein, and raised her eyes to meet his gaze. Then she returned, and the last two to accept her offering were Johndrow and Vanessa.

"Do you know the offertory?" Johndrow asked softly.

Kali nodded. She rose then, and turned to the room.

"Take," she said. "I offer myself freely. Drink. I would share my history, and my future. Know my heart, and those I have shared."

"I accept," Johndrow said. He drank. The others, one by one, repeated his words, and drained their glasses. The room shimmered and faded. The light, so dim it was almost non-existent, glimmered and glowed. Johndrow leaned on the bar, and Vanessa leaned on Johndrow. The others, all but Vein, sat. Kali moved to Vein, slid behind him, and supported him as his eyes glazed.

Then—they remembered.

CHAPTER FOUR

"My becoming," Kali said softly, as the room faded, and they drifted into her past, "was a thing of violence. I lived in a small town with my family. I would have gone on to a different life, a better life. I never had that chance. This is my story..."

Johndrow and the others felt the blood bonding with their own. They felt, and saw, the beginning of the vision as if they shared one set of eyes, and one mind. Kali's words set the scene for them, like the voice of a faraway storyteller. As the story progressed, they knew her voice would fade, and they would join with the memory coded into her blood.

Old Mill, North Carolina, butts up against the Great Dismal Swamp, about an hour and a half from the Outer Banks, where rich families spend their summers riding waves, guzzling beer from the Brew-Thru, and eating expensive seafood in their timeshares and condominiums. To the north, across the Virginia Border, lay Norfolk, Virginia Beach, and farther north, the nation's capital.

Along the old trail of Highway17 runs the Intercoastal Waterway, stretching the length of the east coast down to Florida, providing a path for trade and travel since the days when George Washington was a surveyor. The deeper you venture into the swamp itself, the more you see of what once was, and the less of today remains. There are bears, snakes, some say alligators and even monsters; there are shacks and families far removed from polite society. There are hunters and poachers, hunted men, and drunks. It's a different world, or, possibly, just the same world—but at a point where time moves more slowly.

Old Mill rests on the edges. It's not in the swamp, but neither is it close to any city. There is a grocery store, and a liquor store. There are at least two dozen churches. There is a hardware store, a feed store, and not much more . Three streets, five streetlights, and a wide, spread-out array of small neighborhoods, huge old Colonial style homes, and trailer parks rounded out the town. On one street you can find all three kinds of homes, as well as rundown homes with boarded windows and drug dealers on the porches. Sullen dogs on short, heavy chains guard these, but if you travel three blocks toward the center of town you pass manicured lawns and SUVs. It's a place of contradictions. It lays on a joining of the old world and the new, a crossroad of the great ley lines that stream energy and magic through the earth. It is a place of power, though you'd never guess it from a conversation with most of the inhabitants.

On the outer edge of town sat a small house that had once been blue, but had long since faded to a dark gray. There was a fence around the front, and beds of flowers lined the walls. Though the paint was faded, there was a new roof, and the grass was cut. It was the home of a family who cared about their lives and one another. The father worked on a farm down south near Edenton, driving there each day in his worn pickup truck. The mother ran a cleaning service, aided in the evenings and weekends by her daughter, Alicia. They had a boy, too, who had just started high school. He played football and guitar and, against the odds in that secluded place with little to pass the time, he did not do drugs, drink, or rob those better off and nearer in toward the town's center. He stayed home. He worked with his father when he could. He watched out for his older sister, and though she would never admit it, Alicia loved him for it. Old Mill could be a good place, but it was also rough, and far too close to the dark edges of things. Alicia was a very attractive girl, and she drew notice.

There were no real hotels in the area, but Alicia's mother, Ida, cleaned for many of the well-to-do families in the big houses near the water, and she did regular cleanings for two or three bed and breakfasts run from plantation houses and some of the larger historic homes in town. It was the bed and breakfasts where Alicia's help was needed most, and the two worked them together for long hours. When possible, Alicia's father drove them to and from work in the back of his truck, but on other occasions the two walked, together when possible. When Alicia was forced to walk alone, her brother Alain often accompanied her.

The Boar and the Anchor had been a cotton plantation back in the day. As the cotton mills closed, and the cotton—still grown in the area—was packed onto ships and taken overseas to foreign processing plants, the old families sold out, and a new breed moved in. They turned the great, old homes, once single family residences alive with servants and slaves, into more modern structures. They separated rooms and added facilities. They modernized the kitchens and dining rooms while maintaining as much of the old world charm as possible. They brought in guests from all over the country to experience a piece of the Old South.

The plantation that held The Boar and the Anchor was set back from the highway down a long, winding road that curled back through a stand of trees. The very back end of the property continued the curve, back in toward Old Mill. That property line bordered the crumbling ruin of a very old Quaker church and an ancient cemetery; the far side of that cemetery ran directly along the edge of the swamp. The cemetery had been there a very, very long time. On the far end of it a worn dirt road ended at a rusty gate, and that gate opened onto Queen Street in Old Mill.

The cemetery was a dark place. No one had been buried there for more than a century. There were no flowers left on the graves, and there were rarely visitors, even during the brighter hours of the day. Too many stories had been told over too many years. People disappeared in that place. The police only patrolled Queen Street. They didn't enter the cemetery unless it was necessary, and it was ---more often than they liked. Bodies had turned up there that were never buried. Drug deals had gone bad. Kids looking for a private place to drink beer and have sex had gone missing, or been found murdered and dumped in the weeds.

When Alicia started down Queen Street toward that old rusty gate, Alain balked. He grabbed her arm.

"Are you crazy? You can't go through there. It's only a mile down to the highway, and we can cut over."

"It'll save twenty minutes," Alicia said. "Mama needs me. There's a big party coming in tomorrow. We have to have everything ready, and I don't want to be there late."

"You go through there, and I'm telling Dad," Alain said flatly. "It isn't safe, and twenty saved minutes isn't worth your life."

Alicia laughed. "You believe all those old stories? You know anyone who ever disappeared in the cemetery, Al?"

He frowned and shook his head. "Doesn't matter. Just because I haven't seen it happen doesn't mean it never did. We're walking out to 17."

She sighed and turned, following him away from the cemetery. She knew that he was right, but she hated to be late—and she hated to openly take orders from her younger brother. They didn't speak for the rest of the trip. When Alain turned back to return home, she didn't even wave.

The day was a long one. With evening approaching fast, Alicia and her mother still had two rooms to prepare.

"Dinner is going to be late," Ida fretted.

"You go ahead, Mama," Alicia said. "I can handle these last two rooms, and that way supper will be ready by the time I get home."

"I don't like you walking home alone," Ida said.

"If I can't get someone to drive me, I'll be careful. If I stay out on 17, and then cut through the middle of town, there are lights all along the way. I'll be fine. I'm not a child, you know. You walk home alone almost every day."

Ida met her daughter's gaze. "You have grown into a fine young woman," she said. "I am very proud of you. That doesn't mean a mother isn't going to worry, and there's nothing you can do or say that will ever change it. You're still my baby girl."

Alicia laughed. "Go, mama. I'll be fine."

Reluctantly, her mother agreed, unfastening the ties on her apron. "You get through those two rooms, and come straight home," she said. "I'll be worried until you get there, and you know how your papa is. He'll be out looking for the sheriff in an hour."

Alicia waved her mother on, and continued to the next room. She had to change the sheets, turn down the bed, make sure the towels were fresh and all the extras were carefully placed in the bathroom for the next day's guests. The Boar and Anchor prided itself on customer service.

"It's not how comfortable the beds are, or how good the food is," Old Mr. White was fond of saying. "It's the experience. Things have to be just so. Even if they are nothing like they were a hundred years ago, they have to look like they are. People pay for atmosphere, and we don't want a single out-of-place distraction to spoil it for them."

Alicia worked quickly, but carefully. Her mother had trusted her, and that was something Alicia took seriously. She always tried to do her best for the Whites. They gave her bonuses every Christmas, and little presents when she least expected it. They were quick with a smile and understanding if she was sick. All of that was good. What was better was that she knew her mother was proud of her.

It took longer to do the second room than she'd planned. By the time she'd tucked in the last corner and polished the mirror in the bathroom, the sun was dipping toward the skyline, and she knew she was going to be late. If she got home after dark, her mother's prediction of her father going to the sheriff would be a reality, and she'd be under guard by both father and brother for at least a month.

She left her apron in the cleaning station and slipped out with a smile and wave to Mrs. White, who was manning the desk. There was seldom business this late on a weeknight, but someone was always at that desk, smiling and waiting. It was part of the Boar and Anchor's charm.

She started down the drive toward 17, and then she stopped. Even if she jogged and managed to keep up a good pace, if she went all the way to the highway and around, she was going to be too late. If something happened, or she got winded...

She glanced over her shoulder, thought about it for just a few seconds, and then turned. She took off down the drive toward the back of the plantation house, the swamp, and the cemetery. It wasn't dark yet, and if she hurried, she'd have plenty of light to make her way through the graves and out onto Queen Street. With a little luck, she'd end up home just in time.

She opened the hasp on the old gate, slipped through into the graveyard beyond, and closed it behind her. The iron latch dropped into place with a loud *thunk* that echoed. For just a moment she froze, listening, to see if it would attract anyone, or anything, but there was nothing but silence, and with a soft laugh and a shake of her head, she started off through the graves at a trot.

From the shadows at the edge of the swamp, two baleful, yellow eyes marked her passage. As she moved on toward the older graves in the center of the cemetery, those eyes tracked her, even as the dying light lengthened the shadows and stretched them across her trail like giant groping talons.

CHAPTER FIVE

Alicia's confidence began to slip as she neared the oldest of the graves. In the middle were the tombs and vaults of more than a century past. They'd been built to house provincial governors, explorers, plantation owners, religious men, and entire families. The marble walls and concrete monuments were grimy with mud from the storms and rains of more than a century and green with moss. Some had crumbled, and the tops of crosses and carved angels had toppled and broken.

She knew she should keep running, but something in the air, a thickness, or *wrongness* slowed her down. It felt somehow disrespectful to run in such a place, so, heart pounding, she skittered from stone to stone, wishing she'd gone the other way, or any other way, yearning for the lights of the Red Apple Convenience and Gas out on 17, and the harsh remonstrations of her father. Anything but this.

Then she saw him and she froze.

He was tall. He stood partially in shadow and partially in the wash of moonlight over the white marble wall of a mausoleum. Where the light hit him, his skin gleamed. It seemed almost white, or pearlescent, and smooth like glass. Alicia stopped cold and trembled.

"Who is it?" she asked.

There was no answer. The stranger stood very still, leaning on the stone wall, and watching her. She couldn't see his eyes, but she felt them crawling over her slowly. She took a step forward, and then another. She'd heard the phrase trapped like a deer in headlights before, but had never really understood it. In that moment, wanting more than anything she'd ever wanted to turn and run until her lungs exploded, and to escape, she walked forward slowly, barely able to control the tremors in her limbs, and frightened that if she did run she would not be able to take a deep breath, and that she'd fall, or even pass out, from the effort.

When she took her third step, he moved. It was a deceptive motion. He straightened slowly, stretching like a huge, lazy cat, and then, without any break in time, he stood beside her. He put a hand on her shoulder, and though she tried to pull back away from him, to turn, and to run, and to scream, he held her easily. Just three fingers resting gently on her flesh, and the eyes that had been hidden by shadows, gazing into her own.

"So pretty," he said. "So young and full of life. Where do you run to child? What do you run from?"

Alicia opened her mouth, but no sound came out. Her jaw worked slowly, she closed it and swallowed.

The stranger circled her then, very slowly. She felt his finger trace a line around her throat, one shoulder to the other, and then back, and again he stood before her. He lifted her chin so she met his gaze again.

"Do you know this place?" he asked. "The house of the dead? The names on these graves, these tombs, tell many stories. I could spend a lifetime telling you just the ones I know."

Something released then. It felt physical, as if she'd been restrained, and now, she'd been freed. He still held her chin up with his finger.

"I–I have to go," she said. "My father…"

"Does not know you are in the graveyard," the stranger finished. "In fact, I would be very surprised if anyone had any idea you were here. After all," he chuckled, "they don't know that I'm here, do they? I am always here. Watching."

"Watching what?" she asked.

"Watching over the dead," he said with a shrug. He turned then, back toward the graves. "Watching for visitors. Watching for someone to hear my stories and share my shadows."

The strength had returned to her limbs, but the trembling, if anything, had increased. She had never been so terrified, but still, she hesitated. She was fast. She knew she could run. The graveyard was treacherous. She could fall, hurt herself, break her leg, and he hadn't made a move to hurt her.

"It would do no good," the man said. He didn't turn back to her, but spoke into the shadows. His voice was strange. It seemed to come from all sides at once. She wondered, briefly, if he'd spoken at all, or if she had just heard his thoughts. A breeze lifted her hair and tickled her ear, and it was as if he pressed his lips close and his breath brushed her skin.

"What?" she asked, her voice sounding very small.

"Running," he said. "There is nowhere in this graveyard you could run that I could not catch you."

She caught her breath, and he laughed.

"Surely you knew I would understand your fear? You meet a stranger in the cemetery after dark, and there's no telling who, or what, he might be."

She glanced around and saw that more time had passed than she'd realized. The lengthening shadows had joined and solidified. The sun was no more than an orange red glow, with highlights of purple and gold, sliding down the sky as if melting from some great, cosmic painting.

"Beautiful," he said. "Isn't it? It's the closest I've come to the daylight in a very, very long time—though I am working on that. He turned back to her and held out his hand. "Come, I would like to introduce you to my friends."

She started to run at last. It was too little, and far too late, but she got her legs in motion. She spun and sprinted away from him, making for the Queen Street gate. There was no sound of pursuit, and for a moment she thought—just maybe—that he'd been bluffing. Maybe he wasn't following her at all. Maybe he'd only meant to scare her, teach her the lesson her brother had tried to teach her short hours before. It seemed a lifetime away.

Then he was there, directly in front of her. She tried to dodge to the side and slip around him, but he moved again and she ran into him. She hit hard, and thought surely he would topple over backward or at least that she would bounce off and wind around the side, but he didn't budge. It was like running into a solid wall of ice. He wound his arms around her, and it felt as if the warmth drained from her body in that moment, and all air was sucked from her lungs.

He leaned in then, and this time he did speak directly into her ear.

"It was a polite invitation, girl," he said. "Now I'm afraid you've made it personal."

She didn't feel it as his fangs violated her. Her skin was so cold it burned. She tried to twist, but as she did he pressed his hands into the small of her back and drew her close. Her mind shriveled. She could not scream or speak, but hung paralyzed in his grip. She felt herself flowing up, and out, draining from the point where his lips pressed to her throat. She felt nothing in return. Her struggles were no more than the flutter of a butterfly held by the wings after coming too close to a flame.

She thought of her home. She thought of her mother's arms, and her father. She thought of her bed, and summer days playing in the park by the river with Alain. She thought of the boy she'd kissed after her senior prom and then would have laughed and cried and laughed again at the absurdity that, just like they said would happen, her life was flashing before her eyes.

The night was dark, but what she felt was beyond dark. It was black, no color, and no light, nothing that she understood or knew; there was nothing at all.

Then the man lurched and pulled free. He growled and threw her. She fell, unable to break that fall, or to do anything but watch what happened in slow motion. She saw another shadowy figure. She saw a branch crash into the stranger's face and heard him snarl in fury. Then she heard Alain, and she tried to cry out. She tried to warn him. As the darkness took her, she heard a snap, and a loud crash, and she felt herself lifted like a child and carried away. Away from the prone, lifeless figure face down in the graveyard dirt. Away from Alain's broken body and into the depths of the swamp.

When she woke, there was no light. It wasn't dark in the way it is at night, when the sun has fled from the sky and shadows expand to swallow the world. It was pitch black—absolutely no glimmer of light broke the absolute void that surrounded her. She was cold, colder than she'd ever felt. She tried to move, but she was weak. Her arms and legs were too heavy to move, and even the act of lifting her head was too much. The silence was as complete as the darkness.

She tried to force air up through her throat, to speak or cry out, but at first nothing at all happened. She tried again, and a third time, and that time a tiny gurgle of air wheezed forth. The faintest whisper. There was no way anyone could have heard it, except—he did. He was there before she could try again, before she could try to moisten her lips with a tongue that felt as if it had been blotted for hours with dry cotton. His fingers brushed her cheek. She couldn't see him, but somehow she sensed him and knew him.

Then a very small trickle of something hit her lips. She licked at it weakly like a newborn kitten suckling for milk. She worked it around her mouth, fought to clear the gum holding her lips shut so she could speak, or scream. Too late she realized it was not water that she tasted. It was too thick, coppery, and rich. She tried again to struggle, and tried, just for a moment, to force the blood back out through her lips, but there was more, and it drenched her tongue, and in that instant, something shifted deep inside; something roared up from the center of her being—a hunger she'd never felt. Her struggle to force the flow of warm blood back out of her mouth shifted suddenly and savagely. She drank it in greedily, reached up with a suddenly supple tongue for more, snapped at the air to try and grasp the source and drag it to her.

The corners of her eyes itched, as they always had when tears threatened, but there was no moisture. Nothing trickled down her cheeks, though her chest constricted as it always had, and the pain, more mental than physical, clawed at her. It was more than pain, it was shame, humiliation. She accepted the dribble of blood and would have begged for it—done anything for it.

And still, she fought. Her mind cleared, image by image. She remembered the cemetery. She remembered the stranger, and how he'd taken her. She remembered the struggle and the sounds, Alain's broken body, and then she found her voice.

It bubbled up from deep inside and sprayed the blood up in a fine mist. Even as it escaped, something inside her screamed to have it back, but her voice was stronger. Just for that instant. Just for one word.

"Alain!" she gasped.

A finger brushed over her lips.

"Quiet, little one, you must feed. Your brother no longer needs your concern. He is beyond you. He is even beyond me, but you are not. You must feed, and then you will sleep. While the sun bakes the earth above us, you will sleep. When the night comes again, you will learn. You will hate me for it, but you will learn, and you will come to see them all as I do—cattle. Food. Beneath you.

"It has been a very long time since I had one such as you to share the shadows. I look forward to it. But now..."

He stopped speaking, and before she could try again, he lowered something—his wrist?—to her mouth and she bit hard. It was the strangest sensation she'd ever felt. She tasted the blood, and she snapped tight on the skin with her teeth. She gripped, and something inside her jaw released. She felt it like the snap of a spring. She latched on and it was not like biting had ever been before. Not like chewing or grinding. She pierced him, and the blood flowed, and her memories blanked out again as he allowed her to feed...just for a while. She drifted into dreams, and as the sun rose in places she would never see again in its light, she slept.

CHAPTER SIX

They had found Alain's body many hours before Alicia was able to travel. They'd cleared everything from the cemetery except a sad, flapping outline of yellow tape. They'd looked for her most of the day. She knew this because she could hear them. From so far away that the trees blocked them from her sight, and their voices should have been nothing but whispers in the breeze, she now heard their words clearly. She felt their hearts beating as if they wandered closer to the swamp, and each time she did, she flinched and pulled back. The hunger constricted the muscles of her throat. The one who'd taken her—the dark stranger—had not returned to her.

She'd awakened to a slightly less complete darkness, and she'd had the strength to rise. She was not, as she feared, sleeping in a coffin, a tomb, or a mausoleum. It was a ruined church. She had never seen the place before, it was so far back in the swamp that the roads that had once led to it were gone, overgrown and lost to time. The steeple had fallen. It looked as if it had been struck by lightning, breaking almost directly down the center and toppling like the trunk of some great tree.

The church was surrounded by an even older graveyard than the one where she'd been taken. Most of the names were crumbled and lost to time, though some of the monuments were grand and overbearing. All of it was covered in mold and weeds.

She'd climbed stairs that led up from a stone basement and out through solid, wooden doors. One side of those doors had been opened up and out to allow just a trickle of the evening light to invade the stairwell. Whether or not he'd spent the night with her in the shadows, the stranger was nowhere to be seen. She was more alone than she could ever remember being. She knew that it should frighten her, but she wasn't frightened. She was angry. It burned through her and coursed through her veins and she barely contained the urge to turn her face to the sky and scream.

The sun had still filtered through the trees when she'd risen. A single beam of it had sliced through the doorway beside where she'd stood. She'd avoided it, and when she realized what she'd done, she'd reached for it. She didn't want whatever had been done to her to steal that light. She didn't want her body to change—her mind and her heart and her passion—not without a fight. She'd reached into that light, and her fingers had crisped. Her arm had browned and her skin crackled. She'd pulled back so quickly that she tumbled down the stairs, and even that didn't happen as it should have. She flipped, actually kicked off the wall, and spun in the air to land on her feet at the bottom.

Her arm had burned as if it had been pressed against hot coals. She'd felt the pain, and yet, it was not enough to put her down. It fueled her anger. It drove her hunger deeper—another lesson, she realized, because if she needed to feed on blood to survive, how much more blood would she need to heal? Whose blood? Where would it come from?

And where was he? Where was he with his talk of not having anyone to share the shadows with? If he'd waited so long to have someone to talk to, where was the bastard? Surely not afraid of her, no matter how suddenly powerful she felt. And why, while questions were being asked, had he been able to leave and open that door above her without frying to a cinder?

She had carefully climbed out past the errant sunbeam and sat, leaning against a wall of the ruined church to wait for nightfall. When the shadows stretched across the ruined graveyard, she rose and carefully made her way into the deeper darkness of the swamp and the surrounding woods. There were animals there. She sensed them and almost before she realized it had happened, she'd locked onto a rabbit, chased it down, and fed. She barely had time to feel the revulsion the act brought before the raw need took hold and erased it. She felt it slide away, and that lost pain tore at her on a deeper level, because she sensed it was only a beginning. First the rabbit, and then, how long before the thought of taking a life wouldn't bother her? How long before the loss of her family, her friends, the heat of her body and the life she'd planned faded into the hunger and were nothing more than dim, unimportant dreams to her?

Those thoughts were what brought her to the edge of the cemetery. The fear of that absolute loss tore at her as if hooks were fixed in her soul. She wanted them to be there, all of them. She wanted to run into her father's arms and apologize to him for taking the shortcut. She wanted to beg him to help her, to make it all go away, to call in the sheriff and hunt the dark man through the swamp and destroy him. All of these things she wanted drew her to the cemetery. The crime scene tape, the empty shadows, and the rusty wrought-iron gates, now closed, that led to Queen Street were her new reality.

She knew she could climb the fence. She knew, in fact, though she had no idea how she knew, that she could probably break the lock and go through the gate. She could go to her father, and, on some level, she suspected that the dark man hoped she would. What would happen then? She knew what she wanted to believe, but she did *not* believe it. They would see her, and she would be as he was. She was, what, dead? Undead? And Alain? She was pretty sure her brother was dead too, trying to save her. At least he'd been spared this. And there it was, her mind already shifting to a new perspective where the horror became almost matter-of-fact.

As she watched, a figure peeled itself from the shadows of Queen Street. Alicia froze. Her senses reached out before she could catch herself, and she felt the heat of fresh blood. She also caught the woman's familiar scent. One slow, painful step at a time, her mother drew closer. The itching burn at the edges of Alicia's eyes that had replaced tears nearly overwhelmed her, followed by a wave of hunger so intense she had to press her hands into the tree she leaned on so hard, her nails broke through the trunk to prevent herself from rushing the fence.

Her mother didn't see her. Alicia focused all of what was left of herself on beating back the hunger. She retreated, one step, and then another. She glanced up and somehow, across the cemetery through the bars of the gate her gaze penetrated the darkness, and she sensed, for a heartbeat, that her mother met that gaze. Then she realized that the heartbeat she heard was her mother's, and that if she listened for another, she might lose control. She uttered a strangled, tortured cry that might have been an animal, or a bird, and turned back to the swamp.

She ran and ran. Along the way she came upon a doe, beautiful and alone in the moonlight. She saw the whites of its eyes as it sensed her, saw the twitch in its muscles and heard the hammering, thudding magic of the blood pumping through its veins. She ran, and she dove, and she fed.

When it was done, she slunk back through the woods and the trees and the swamp to the church. She found what had been one of the pews, broken and rotted from the weather, and she sat, facing the spot where the altar would have been, wondering if, if she prayed, lightning would end her once and for all and silence the pain.

As she sat there, silent and unmoving, he returned. That was how it began.

CHAPTER SEVEN

The mental bond snapped, and Johndrow pulled back with a soft cry. He'd experienced the sharing before but never with such intensity, or with such a large group. He'd expected a few images, and possibly an impression of Kali's sire. What he'd experienced filled him with wonder, and with dread, because the worst they'd feared was what they'd found. Her creator was old, very, very old, and something more. If what Johndrow had read was correct, the creature was not entirely a vampire. It walked in the twilight, and the sunrise. Possibly not in the full light of day, but even the advantage of an hour of light for one of his kind was dangerous. This was worse.

He shook his head, backed up against the bar, and steadied himself. Around him, the others, each in their particular way and with varying degrees of ability, returned to their own thoughts and senses. Only Kali stood her ground, and Vein, who must already have shared, and have known what was to come.

"My God," Joel said. "Who…what was that?"

"He was old," Vanessa said, wonder in her voice. "Old and…"

"And not fully a vampire," Johndrow finished. "I have no idea on the 'who,' because it's no one we've associated with. I've heard rumors of ancients who were able to stay abroad in twilight, but nothing like this."

"His name," Kali said, her voice clear and dark, "is Starkey. George Starkey. He was an alchemist, a very powerful man, when he came to the blood. He lost that power, but not the knowledge. He was more than a man, and now, he is more than a vampire. It changes nothing.

"He took my family. He killed my brother, Alain, that first night in the cemetery. He killed my father a week later when he came too close to tracking us. He bound me and killed my mother as I watched, and then, knowing I could not fight him, he made me feed on her blood. He stole my world, and for that, I will end his."

"It cannot be done," Johndrow said softly. "No matter how much you hate, in the night he is more powerful than any of us—possibly more than all of us together. In the hours just before, and after? He walks, and you must sleep. It cannot be done."

Kali lowered her eyes to the floor, just for a moment, and then she raised them again. "I hurt him once, and I escaped. I did that by myself. If I must do this alone, I will do it, but I have no choice. Of all the elders, you understand that. We have shared, and I know."

Johndrow met her gaze. He knew she spoke the truth, but he had read in the eyes of all the others, and their silence, how they would stand. The High Council would not challenge a power that might actually challenge them in return. They'd been complacent far too long for such an endeavor, and who would they send? Even with a plan—with carefully executed attacks—they stood only a small chance of success. Still, he wanted to help.

"You must leave us now," he said. "The Council will contact you with our decision. You will not have long to wait."

"So we are—dismissed?" Vein said, stepping forward. His eyes flashed dangerously, but Kali controlled him with a hand on his arm.

"We will go," she said. "I think we've already had all the answers we will get."

She turned, and she strode from the room, her head held high. Vein met Johndrow's gaze a moment longer, then turned and followed. His companions filed out after him-- a sullen, silent army.

Vanessa slipped away from Johndrow's side also.

"Where are you going?" he asked.

She turned back, and her eyes flashed, but she controlled her emotions. "I will see them out, and then I will return for the vote."

She turned, and she was gone, and Johndrow stood silent in the center of the room, aware that the others watched him closely. He held his silence. Vanessa's departure granted him a few moments to think, and he wasn't quite ready to face what he could not help but think of as the group cowardice of his peers. He watched the door through which Vanessa had departed, and he waited.

Vanessa stepped into the hall before Kali or the dark man running security reached the elevator.

"Wait," she said. She spoke softly, but they all turned; Vein turned first, because of the blood bond. She hurried up behind them and took Kali's hands, ignoring the others.

"I knew what would happen here tonight," she said. "Johndrow and I would help—will help—but it won't be with the Council's approval or assistance, unless I've read them wrong. There are others you can call on. The woman, Amethyst, is holding things for you—things I've asked her to find. The first is a more powerful bloodstone, and one that is charmed so that the one you seek can't use it to track back to you. There are other things, but I wish there was more.

"The one you face is more than a vampire. He is undead, but I sense he is patient, powerful, and intends to live again. He intends to walk by day, and though it should be impossible…he has made a start."

"Anyone—anything—can be killed," Kali said flatly. "I almost killed him. He will remember me."

"He is also bound to you, and you to him," Vanessa said sharply. "I know you will do this thing no matter what anyone else might wish for you, so listen to me now while you have the chance. Don't go in blind. Don't turn away help from any quarter. Look for an advantage. You're going to need it. Victory isn't going to come from your anger, and it isn't going to come from your speed, or your strength. He knows them; he's stronger, and faster. You know him, that's true. He knows you as well. You can't act as he will expect you to, and you can't attack him as you might a peer. He will end you, or worse, take you back and make you his toy again.

"Go to the woman, Amethyst. Get what I have left for you, and wait for the others to make their decision. Plan. Think of assets you would normally not consider. It is one thing to go on an impossible quest; heroes and fools have done this since the beginning of time. There is a difference between foolish and stupid. You will hear from me soon."

She turned then and didn't wait for an answer. She was slender and tall, old and proud, and though all of those she left in that hall wanted to say something, to puff out their chests and tell her she was wrong, none of them moved until she'd rounded the corner and stepped from sight. Then they turned, security accessed the elevator, and they left in silence.

Vanessa returned to Johndrow's side and wrapped her arm around his back. The symbolism was lost on no one. She'd gone to the young ones on their way out, she was blood bonded to them, and she and Johndrow stood as one.

"So," Joel cut the silence. "I do not believe I am the only one who did not expect that. I can't say that knowing such a being walks the Earth sits well with me. It smacks too much of the type of imbalance that nearly stole Vanessa from us so recently—only this time, it is one of our own crossing lines."

"If that is true," Nystrom cut in, "he has been crossing those lines longer than some of us have known the blood. I have never felt anything like that. And the sunlight…I felt it when she touched it, and I saw the open door. How is that possible?"

"For you?" Lydia cut in. "For me? It is not possible. It is never going to happen in a million years of sunrises, and that should be fine. There are prices to be paid for the powers that we share, and for the blood."

"Truer words have never been spoken," Johndrow said. He turned to the bar, pulled down the wine he'd originally intended to serve, and without ceremony uncorked it. He poured, and Vanessa carried the glasses around the room. They needed to clear their minds and that meant washing away Kali's memories as swiftly, and as completely as possible.

Glass in hand, he turned back to address the room.

"If this were just what it seemed on the surface," he said, "I would have to say, the young ones are on their own. Blood quests are personal. In the end, any serious assistance in such an endeavor would lead to resentment down the road. This, though, this is no ordinary creature we are talking about. This is a threat to the balance of things and in particular to the balance that is ours—the blood—the night—the lives we live and covet and try so hard to protect. This is one of our *own* breaking rules that were never meant to be broken, and it will not go unnoticed. It might not be now, maybe not even this century, but as he works toward this goal of his—a goal he does not, by the way, share with others of his kind—he will draw attention. There are many powers in the world, and many of them have a dim view of imbalance."

"Then," Nystrom said, "let one of them make it right. Let them find this Starkey and end him. No need for us to be involved."

"You are involved," Johndrow said, turning to face Nystrom with an icy gaze, "because he is one of us. There are uneasy truces all over the world. Some are with mortals, some are with wizards, others are between creatures and races we aren't even aware of. They are going to look at this as a problem that falls on us. If we don't solve it, they are going to think either we support what he is doing, or that we don't believe we have to police our own. They may think, *what if another of those 'bloodsuckers' gets it in his head to play God? Maybe we should just teach them a lesson now and make sure it sticks.* There are greater wars than this will be, and I'm here to tell you if we can't face this problem, we are in no way ready for those others."

It was a shot in the dark. He knew what he said was true, and that lent his words power, but he knew the others as well, and he knew that, no matter what he said or did, they would serve their own interests in what was to come. He didn't believe he could make them fight, but wanted them to leave his home with the knowledge of their responsibility, and their cowardice. It was something he could play on, if things went badly.

He knew that he would do what he could. He wasn't going to take off across country to attack one of the ancients, but he had resources, he had contacts, and he would make use of every one of them before this was through. If things went very, very badly, he would drag these frightened old women back into the night, and they would hunt. It had been many years—seemingly lifetimes away from the present—but he was able to recall these lifetimes without being overwhelmed.

"We should not abandon our own," he said. "The young ones are blood bonded to my Vanessa. We could lend support. What say you?"

Nystrom spoke up immediately.

"I'm out," he said. "It's not our fight. It's not even a fight, unless she makes it one. It is in no way connected to us, until we make the connection. That won't be coming from me."

Lydia nodded in agreement. "We are a very long way from North Carolina," she said. "There's been no threat to our own, and there is no indication that he will come after her. The risk is too great."

Johndrow wanted to rail at them. Every second he listened to this, his own rich, comfortable existence closed in on him more tightly. He felt as if the second life he'd been given was being squeezed out of him.

"I almost wish that I could go," Joel said wistfully. "I have the bank, and I know if I left, Ligaya would go as well," he smiled up at his taller, beautiful lover. "There is no one I can trust in my absence, and there are too many counting on me to risk not coming back. It's the cost of the material world intruding, I suppose. If it matters to any of you, I support this in my heart."

"It matters to me, old friend," Johndrow said, clasping Joel on the shoulder.

One by one, the others made their excuses, made their apologies, and proclaimed their disinterest. Johndrow knew that the time was coming when the Council would only exist in name. They gathered socially, but they never acted. Even when Vanessa had been captured and nearly destroyed, it was all he could do to get them to support his efforts to get her back. He even thought it was time he and Vanessa did some traveling of their own. The building was too much like a giant, secure coffin.

"I thank you all for gathering," he said. "It has been an enlightening evening, in many ways."

Nystrom glanced at him, searching his expression for some insult. He kept himself in check and neutral.

"We will gather again soon, I trust. There are always matters needing our attention. Perhaps, when this business is over, we can hear the report. Assuming there are survivors to tell it."

"You would do well," Corwyn said, "to talk her out of it. The anger will fade. All emotion fades with time. You know this, as well as I. She does not have to destroy herself for her rage."

"I suppose not," Johndrow said. "It would truly be a shame if any of us were impertinent enough to try and make a mark on the world. After all, we are just shadows, yes?"

They all looked at him then. Several of them wanted to speak, but catching the sudden glitter in his eyes, held their silence. They filed out slowly. Joel and Ligaya were the last, and Johndrow forced himself to relax his anger and bid his friend farewell."

"We must hunt soon," he said softly. "I remember…better days."

"All things flow in cycles," Joel said. "There will come a time, my friend, when we will have our chance to change the world. Again. If you believe nothing else, believe that."

Johndrow nodded.

"I'm calling DeChance," he said. "I should have suggested it in the meeting, but I'm afraid even that much support is beyond that group. I will pay, of course, but I have to do something."

Vanessa laughed then, and hugged him. She leaned up, kissed him on the cheek, and smiled brightly.

"But…I have already spoken to Donovan," she said. "Did I forget to mention it?"

They stared at her a moment, and then, as a group, they burst into laughter. "I knew," Johndrow said, "there was a reason I love you beyond… all of this." He swept his gaze down her form appreciatively. "You never cease to surprise and amaze me."

"I hope," she said, "that I never will. And never is a very long time."

CHAPTER EIGHT

Donovan sat across the table from Amethyst in a booth in the back of Big Sid's in downtown San Valencez. The food was standard fare for a club: burgers, sandwiches, re-heated entrees and house wine in carafes that had seen better days. Sid's was a place you met for one of two or three reasons. None of those reasons was the food.

The club boasted some of the best live entertainment in the state. No one knew how he did it year after year, but Sid drew in some great bands, a lot of old bluesmen on the road and rock legends slumming with off-name bands for a holiday. There had even been stars born there. The band Maelstrom had played there, back in the day. There was a blues guitarist named Brandt who'd made local waves a few years back, then disappeared into the mountains with his band. Donovan had heard rumors that they were still around, and the rumors were interesting, but they were for another day. He and Amethyst had also not come for the music, which didn't start for another hour.

Sid's was also a good place to meet if you had things to discuss you didn't need the rest of the world overhearing. The back wall was lined with heavily upholstered booths. There were fans, and bottles clinking, pool tables by day and music by night, and if Sid knew you, you could count on a modicum of privacy. Donovan had known Sid a very long time.

"So," she said, "Vanessa came to you too?"

Donovan smiled as he detected a wary tone in her voice. They were both well aware of the ancient vampire's allure, and the blood bond strengthened it.

"She did," he said. "It was an interesting visit, to say the least. I have never seen her without Johndrow present—at least not since…"

Amethyst nodded. "I know. It's a unique situation to say the least. She paid a lot of money for the bloodstone she bought. It's one of the finest I've ever had. I guess it surprises me because I haven't had that many dealings with the undead. I've always considered vampires pretty cold and distant. She obviously cares what happens to this girl, Kali."

"Not her so much, though that may come," Donovan said. "It's Vein. She is Vein's creator, and he is bonding to Kali. Since Vein will go on this fool's errand as well, Vanessa feels bound to do what she can. If it weren't for their places on the High Council, I believe Johndrow and Vanessa would go along and help."

"That would certainly simplify it for us," Amethyst said, taking a bite of her burger. "The money they are offering is good, but I can't help feeling like we've been asked to go on a long trip as chaperones."

"It's more than that," Donovan said. "I mean, that's it, on the surface, but I did a little digging, and I think there's more to it. This isn't your garden-variety vampire Kali is after. He's old. I spoke with Johndrow last night. They did a sharing—he was hoping to draw the others in, build some support—so he convinced Kali to share a few drops of her blood, and thus her memories, with the Council. He got a lot more than he bargained for. He and the others believe that this vampire is one of the ancients."

"That's not good," Amethyst said. "There aren't supposed to be any of those on this continent. And, since when do they hang around in graveyards and steal young girls? I thought the really old ones were beyond that sort of thing. Withdrawn?"

"He's not as old as they think," Donovan said. "They felt his power, and they made assumptions based on their limited experience. I try to never base my decisions on first impressions, because people, and creatures and demons, all have one thing in common—they work very hard to impress. If they are good at it, you can be fooled."

"And the members of the High Council were all fooled?" Amethyst asked. She raised one eyebrow, an expression that Donovan loved, and took a sip from her beer. "Can I be there when you tell them?"

"Don't get me wrong. They aren't fools. He is old, probably older than any on the Council, but he is not an ancient. He was born George Starkey, back in the 1600s. He, theoretically, went to England and died in London during the Black Plague in 1665."

"Wow, he even makes you seem young."

Donovan laughed. "He wasn't just a man, Amethyst, he was an alchemist, possibly the last of the great alchemists. They have never been able to link him to the work, but he is credited as being the actual writer of the works of Eirenaeus Philalethes."

Amethyst perked up. "Isn't he the one they say inspired Sir Isaac Newton?"

"One and the same. He wrote a lot of alchemical texts. I have most of them, including a few that are apocryphal and at least one written by hand and never published."

"And you think he's a vampire?"

"I'm nearly certain," Donovan said. "I called an old friend after Vanessa's visit. You know him—Geoffrey Bullfinch."

"Calling out the big guns, eh?" Amethyst said. "You only consult Bullfinch when things are very obscure."

"We all have our areas of expertise," Donovan said. "Geoffrey is probably the world's foremost expert in myths and folklore. I only called because of the area. This town, Old Mill, lies on the crossing of a major ley line with several smaller ones. There have been a lot of strange things going on there in recent years, and I've heard of a few. It's impossible to keep up on everything though. You know about the organization he works with now?"

"I've heard, yes," Amethyst replied. "O.C.L.T., or something like that? Call me cynical, but when the government gets involved in our world, it's a bad match."

"The vote is still out on that," Donovan said, "but they do have a vast information network. What would have taken me weeks of phone calls, trips to the library, and Internet searches will take him a couple of days. On top of that, as soon as I explained what we seemed to be up against, before I knew it was Starkey, he guessed. Apparently our friend is no more acceptant of his undead status than he was of his mortality. They aren't sure how he's done it, but Starkey has made progress toward walking by day. Kali reported that he was out and about around sunrise, and also that he was mobile much earlier in the day than any undead I've encountered.

"If he's managed to find a way to put his alchemical knowledge to work on this problem, and is making progress, it might explain why he is growing bolder. There were reports he'd returned to America, and even that he was seen in the area of The Great Dismal Swamp, and along the intercoastal waterway. He was thought to have gone to ground—withdrawn, as the ancients have done. It's been over a century since anyone has seen him, or it had been before he took Kali."

"So what changed?"

"I think he's going crazy," Donovan replied. "I believe that he became one of the undead willingly. He wanted more time. He wanted time to finish the work he knew would elude him in a single lifetime. As it turns out, it continues to elude us all, though some believe that the entire process is more allegorical, and that some have attained that perfection."

Amethyst smiled. She glanced down and sipped her beer. Donovan growled, and then laughed

"Okay, sorry. The point is that what he's doing goes against the grain of his nature. If he's walking during daylight it's going to have consequences. There is a …"

"Balance in everything," Amethyst finished. She grinned at him and Donovan was unable to hide his smile.

"Yes. A balance. He has begun to tip that balance and it threatens his existence. The undead exist in darkness because they must, yes, but also because it protects them. It gives them another world to rule. They have their good, and their bad seeds. In that, they aren't much different from those of us who walk by day. The older they grow, in general, the less the undead interact with anything that is not of their world. Their hunger doesn't die, but it fades. They slow, and eventually, or so the legends say, they return to a version of sleep that is like death. That is how it has always been."

"But Starkey has broken that mold," she said.

Donovan nodded. "Instead of pulling away from the sun, and the day, he is trying to embrace it. His actions are not those of an ancient, but of a younger vampire. That means…"

"That Kali won't be the last victim."

"It could get very bad before he's stopped," Donovan said. "Eventually, he'll show himself, and man is a very resilient beast. When darkness steps into bright sunlight, it eventually dissipates, no matter how hard it tries to blot out the sun. He will do something that draws too much attention, and they will destroy him. The question is, before that happens, how many will he kill? How many more like Kali might he create, stealing them from loved ones and families?"

"For that matter," Amethyst said, "how many might he have already created? How many will we actually face, and will they be dangerous, or turn on him?"

"He's too powerful for that," Donovan said. "Without some charms, and a lot of help, Kali won't be able to resist him either, once she gets in close. There is the fact that she hurt him once before. She has been very secretive about that. It wasn't part of the sharing, and Johndrow has no idea what she might have done. She may be holding that back, hoping that what worked once will work again and give her an edge. I've asked Vanessa to try and get Vein to find out what it is. Anything we can learn that gives us an advantage might be important before all is said and done."

"So, what's the plan?" Amethyst asked. "I assume we have one?"

"It's a work in progress," Donovan said. "I need you to trail Kali and the others, or, at least, to parallel their trip. Vanessa is just as worried that Vein can't handle a solo trip across the country without getting himself staked, or worse, as she is about the final outcome. They will be driving, so they won't be making too good of time. I also know the locations of the safe houses they've been granted use of."

"If I'm following the kids, where are you going?" Amethyst asked.

"I'm going on to North Carolina. Bullfinch is there, dealing with something near Asheville. He's promised he'll have more for us, and I think on this one we're going to need everything we can get. You'll be able to reach me, of course, and, within limits, I can travel very quickly."

"You sure know how to show a girl a good time," Amethyst sighed. "Here I thought we were going to vacation in the Great Dismal Swamp, and you're running off for a boy's night out and leaving me with the kids."

"I won't be long," he said. "You could take the train."

"I might do that," she said. "I've always wanted to take one of those sleeper cars across the country. I'm a sucker for a good western."

"They've changed a little," Donovan laughed, "but it beats driving, and it allows you to track them more easily. If you flew, you might end up too far ahead, and have to circle back. Vein is a bit sharper than he was the last time we interacted with him, but he's still rash, arrogant, and this will be his first time on his own so far from the Council, and Vanessa. There are a lot of things besides ancient vampires who could take him out…I'm hoping he'll care enough about Kali, and her quest, to avoid confronting them. I'm hoping, but…"

"You're an incurable optimist." Amethyst finished.

"You have to stop that," Donovan laughed. "One more thing—could you take Cleo with you? I am going to be traveling fast, and it will be easier for me if I have Asmodeus. He can forage for his own food, and I feel safer letting him fly free."

"Of course," Amethyst smiled. "Cleo and I could use some bonding time. I'm going to get her to tell me all your secrets."

"You know more of those than anyone alive," he said, suddenly serious. "We'll have to leave tomorrow, but…"

"Why don't you pay the tab," Amethyst said. "The night is young."

They drained their beers, rose, and Donovan left a twenty on the table. They crossed the still-empty dance floor and slipped out into the falling darkness. No one even glanced up as they departed. Sid's might be a dive, but it could keep secrets.

CHAPTER NINE

Vein stood beside the door to Johndrow's garage and watched as Bruno pulled a black sedan out onto the street. The windows were tinted so deeply they were more like sheets of obsidian than glass. Kali slipped up behind Vein and put her arms around his waist. She leaned her head on his shoulder.

"I can't believe we're finally going," she said. "If I'd had to spend another night hanging out at Club Chaos and thinking about—him—I would have killed something and really gotten us in trouble."

Vein wrapped an arm around her.

"We just have to do this right," Vein said. "I checked all the options. We could have gotten pretty close by train—the Council has special cars that can be included if they give enough notice. I considered it, but we'd have been stuck in some ridiculous hole called Rocky Mount, North Carolina. I checked the map—I don't see the mount. It would be several hours to the closest safe house, and then we'd still have to find a way to get around. It's better if we take the car."

Bones, Shade, and Pierce stepped out of the garage and closed the door behind them.

"I don't see why we're not all going," Pierce said.

"Quit whining," Vein said. "That's your answer, by the way. I can't imagine more than a thousand miles listening to that. It's not like we're leaving forever."

"Hope not," Shade said. He hung back. It was obvious he didn't like being excluded either, but unlike Pierce, he wasn't about to let it show. "Night would be pretty dull here without you two."

Vein had decided it would be best if they traveled in a tighter group. He chose Bruno, who had the advantage of looking physically the oldest, and who was good behind the wheel, and Bones to accompany them. Bones was nearly as old in the blood as Vein himself, and while none of them was an elder by any stretch, he was the best choice of the others when it came down to a fight. He was also a bit smarter, and as arrogant as he was, Vein knew the task they'd set themselves was not only difficult, but possibly beyond their ability.

"Let's get going," he said. "We have a stop to make on the way out, and I want to get as many miles behind us tonight as possible. If we can get over the mountains and down into Nevada, we have a place to hole up."

"Vein!"

They all turned to see Johndrow exiting the main entrance of the huge building. Vanessa hung off his arm. The two of them were so closely attuned that they even walked as a single unit. It was a spectacular sight, and the younger vampires took it in with admiration, being careful to hide it.

"I thought you'd forgotten us," Vein said.

He stepped forward and held out a hand. Johndrow took it, and the two shook.

"If it were simply up to me," Johndrow said, "you'd have the full support of the Council. There may come a time when things are run differently, but for now…"

"I know," Vein said. "I don't think Kali wants anyone else taking out the big bad anyway. We'll be along for moral support."

"Be careful," Vanessa said. "This is going to be like nothing you've ever encountered. He's older than I am, and I'm one of the oldest you're likely to meet in this world. He is powerful, and he will feel the blood bond as you do. You will have to surprise him in some way, and your existence will likely depend on figuring that out before you get there."

"I know some things about him," Kali said softly. "I know where he goes, how he feeds. I know what he will try to do, as well. He is not only old and powerful—he is crazy. It makes him unpredictable, but at the same time, it gives us an advantage."

"Crazy men hold all the cards," Johndrow said. "What matters to one who lives by logic, or reason, will not matter to him. His motivation will be difficult to read. Keep yourselves separated enough that you can strike from more than one direction. Choose the place of battle carefully."

"We've been over this," Vein said. He stepped forward impulsively and hugged Vanessa, who returned the embrace. He turned and actually bowed to Johndrow, who nodded in return, touched in spite of himself. He felt the blood bond too, through Vanessa. It just wasn't as strong.

"Stay in contact," Vanessa said. "All of the safe houses have been readied, and you have cell phones. I don't expect to be sitting here waiting and worrying until you return."

"Yes mom," Vein said, laughing and ducking back. "Now, we have to go."

Bones slid into the front seat beside Bruno, and Vein opened the back door for Kali. She turned, before climbing in, and followed Vein's example, embracing Vanessa.

"Thank you," she said.

She pulled a chain around her neck and drew forth the blood crystal dangling there. It shivered and slid very slightly toward Vein. Vanessa caught it, and smiled.

"It is a very powerful, sensitive crystal," she said. "It will help you to locate your quarry. I see that the blood bond is complete," she added, and she smiled. "You are welcome to my family. I will be pleased to know you when you return."

The formal acceptance silenced them all, for a moment. Vein had known that his bonding with Kali had progressed, but until the crystal moved, he hadn't been certain it was complete. He stared at it in wonder, then shook his head and returned to the moment. Kali slipped the crystal back beneath her black T-shirt and ducked into the back seat. Vein closed the door and crossed to the far side.

"We will see you soon," he said.

Johndrow nodded. "Good hunting," he said.

Then Vein was in the car, Bruno pulled away from the curb, and the four disappeared into the growing darkness. On the sidewalk, Johndrow turned, as if noticing Pierce and Shade for the first time. Their shoulders were slumped, and they looked lost. Johndrow glanced at Vanessa, who nodded.

"So," Johndrow said, "would you gentlemen care for something to drink?"

They stared at him, then at one another, and finally, Shade nodded.

Johndrow led them inside, Vanessa once more blending in as he moved. A few moments later, the street was empty.

Bruno parked on the street outside Donovan's building. He killed the engine, but when Vein and Kali climbed out, he stayed behind the wheel. Bones stayed put as well.

"We'll be back soon," Vein said. "I'd have come by here sooner, but I didn't want Johndrow to know I was asking for help."

Bruno nodded. Bones looked bored.

Vein and Kali entered the building together and walked straight to the elevator. They stepped inside, and as the door closed, Vein studied the panel. There were twenty-two floors in the building, or so it seemed at first glance. Closer inspection showed that, as in many older buildings, the number thirteen did not appear. That would mean there were only twenty-one floors, and Vein smiled.

"There is no button," he said. "He would not miss the chance for his building to have twenty-two floors. The number of letters in the Hebrew alphabet. The number of major Arcana cards in a Tarot deck. How–?"

The elevator started to move. The crystal under Kali's shirt shifted slightly against her skin. She brought her hand up to it, and Vein caught the gesture. He looked up, as though his vision could pierce the walls and floors.

"The blood," he said at last. "It is the strangest thing, but he is bound to me…to you. He is bound to Vanessa, and I do not believe, in all the years of our kind, that something of this sort has occurred. I've heard all the old stories, learned the lore and memorized the rituals. There is no mention of such a bond."

They rode in silence then, and when the elevator stopped, they stepped out. They saw a single door across from them in the center of a long hall. There was a shimmer, some sort of glamour, that suffused the walls.

"A mortal would see doors," Kali said. "I can almost make out their outlines…"

Vein stepped up to the one clearly defined door and raised his hand to knock. Before he could bring his knuckle to the wood, the door opened, and Donovan stood framed in the doorway, illumined by a soft violet light behind him.

"Welcome," he said.

They stepped inside, and Donovan closed the door behind them. Cleo sat on the desk, her tail flipping from side to side, watching carefully. She knew what Vein and Kali were, but she knew Donovan as well. If he did not fear them, and invited them in, she trusted them as well.

"You found something for us?" Vein asked, getting straight to the point. "I know the Council wouldn't come to you on our behalf—they don't support Kali's quest. They were pretty clear about how outgunned we are in this battle…I thought you might be able to help."

Donovan nodded. "I'm glad you came. As you are well aware, taking on one of your kind is never an easy task. It's doubly difficult when there is a blood bond, because it robs you of your most important advantage–surprise. As luck would have it, that is one area in which I think I can be of help. I've prepared some things for you. It's not much, but it's what I could do on short notice. I hope it will be enough."

Kali touched his arm.

"I appreciate what you are doing. When we first met, we were foolish."

"I tend to let the past be what it is," Donovan replied. "We all survived, we learned things. We are friends."

He glanced at Vein then, as if testing the strength of his own remark.

"We are," Vein said. "You ever find yourself on the wrong street after dark, we've got your back, magic man."

Donovan grinned. "Good to know."

He stepped to his desk and retrieved a leather box. He flipped open the top and turned it so that Vein and Kali could see what was inside. There were four small, smoky crystals on gold chains inside.

"What are they?" Vein asked.

"They are shields," Donovan replied. "Since I have the pleasure of sharing your…bond…I was able to use that energy to form them. What they do is very simple. When you wear them, you will be cut off from those you are bonded to. When you wear these, he will not be able to detect you. You will also not feel—your joining—but you don't have to wear them until you are close. It might give you the advantage you need—the chance at a moment of surprise. It might even be a good idea *not* to wear them at first. If he knows you are coming, tracks you across the country even, then you are just gone…"

"It's a good idea, and we'll do it," Vein said. "There is no way we can make the entire trip with these…"

He looked at Kali, and Donovan saw deep emotion in the glance. The young vampire had it bad, and it made him smile. The creatures standing before him, between them, had seen more than a hundred and fifty years, but it still felt like dealing with teenagers. Of course, he was older, so the comparison wasn't far off…but still.

"There is more," he said.

He returned to his desk and came back with a wrapped parcel. It was bound in strips of silk, and tied with leather straps.

"There is a paste in this," he said. "It is deadly to your kind. You have got to be VERY careful with this. I doubt your Council would approve of its existence, and normally I wouldn't deal in it, but I was able to get my hands on this, and I thought it might come in handy. Normal weapons are not going to work, and the things that you fear—the things that could destroy you? They won't work as well on the one you seek. He is stronger than you, faster than you, and more resilient. Just hurting him will get you killed. If you use this on your weapons, even a lucky hit might take him down. If you get him down, you need to use this to keep him there. All of it. When you are done, whatever is left, we will destroy."

"Where did you get such a thing?" Vein asked. He glanced uneasily at Donovan.

"I took it from someone who would have used it," Donovan said simply. "I believe that's called killing two birds with one stone. It's off the street, so your people need not fear it, and at the same time, it may serve a better purpose than it was created for. It's simply about…"

"Balance," Kali finished. She laughed, and both men stared at her.

"When I picked up the blood crystal from your lady," Kali said, "She told me a little about you. About what you do. At first it sounded like mumbo jumbo, but then I thought about it. I thought about what Johndrow said when I—when *we*—shared. It makes sense that one thing balances out against another, that each piece of a puzzle only fits in one place, and when forced into another, causes problems across the entire pattern. I think I'm glad you're here, magic man," she said. "When this is all over, the four of us are going to have to go have a drink."

Donovan frowned and raised an eyebrow.

"Wine!" Kali said. She laughed again, and Donovan found he liked her.

"That is a date," he said. "You are leaving tonight?"

"Now," Vein said. "We want to get across the mountains tonight."

"You know you can call me," Donovan said. "You have my number."

"You know it, magic man," Vein said. "After all, weird as it is—and between you and me, I've never felt anything weirder—we're family, right?"

The two turned then, and Vein opened the door. Kali slipped out, glancing over her shoulder and smiling at Donovan.

"Thank you again," she said.

Then the door closed, and he stood alone in his apartment, wondering why he actually felt worried about the two of them. And wondering about family. He turned and raised an eyebrow at Cleo.

“It has to be on your side,” he said.

She stretched and eyed him, then meowed loudly, turned her back, and lay down to sleep. With a sigh, Donovan went to his room to pack. He had a long trip ahead too, and it didn’t look like sleep was in the cards anytime soon.

CHAPTER TEN

Donovan and Amethyst stood together on the platform, watching as the single brilliant eye of the approaching train wound around the last corner and slowed. He had his arm around her, holding her tightly against him. Her bags sat on the ground at their feet, along with a cat carrier that held a very disgruntled Cleo. She hated to be confined, but, as Donovan had explained, the conductor wasn't going to allow her on the train if she was free.

"I wish you were coming with me," she said. "I love trains, but they aren't anywhere near as fun with no one to share."

"I won't be any longer than I have to be," he said. "I should be able to catch up well before you actually reach North Carolina. For one thing, I'm fairly certain we can't trust our boy Vein to behave for that long. I'm sure he'll find a way to slow them down. Besides, you won't actually be alone, will she, Cleo?"

"Being lonely isn't what I'm worried about," Amethyst said. "Without you along, there's only me and Cleo to keep them out of trouble, and that's no easy task."

"Somehow I think you'll find a way," Donovan said. "I'm sure they'll remember what happened to them in that alley not that long ago when you were angry, and there were two more of them then. Besides, for good or ill, we're bonded to them. I think if push comes to shove, they'll listen to you. In any case, I'm only a phone call away, and as you know, within certain limitations, I can travel very quickly."

She turned and drew him down into a long, slow kiss.

"You just be sure you don't let Bullfinch draw you into his little graveyard problem. We're going to need you—maybe not before we get to Old Mill, but no way am I going up against this 'Starkey' alone, or with a pile of wanna-be punk vampires."

"Yes ma'am," Donovan said.

The train pulled up with a squeal of metal on metal and a whoosh of brakes. The doors opened and Donovan gave Amethyst a last, tight hug.

"Take care of yourself," he said. "I will see you down the road. Try not to get bored on the train."

"I brought plenty of reading material," she said. "You aren't the only one with books or contacts. I'll be boning up on the undead and alchemy and planning what I'll need to be effective against either, or both. I'd like to think you didn't just want me along as a cat-sitter, or for my stunning good looks..."

Donovan's smile widened. "Well, now that you mention it..."

Cleo meowed angrily, and they both laughed.

"Get going, Donovan, before you say something you'll regret," she said. Then, with a smile and a little wave, she grabbed her carry-on bag in one hand and Cleo's crate in the other and stepped up onto the train. Donovan stood and watched until the door closed behind her, and, with a loud warning whistle, the engine whisked her, and the train, off toward the East.

"Go with all the Gods in your pockets, and my heart in your hand," he whispered, breathing the old charm into his hands and then spreading them so he flung his breath after the speeding train.

Then he turned and left the platform, returning through the busy station to the streets beyond with his single, ancient leather duffel bag in hand.

The train station was on the outskirts of San Valencez, north of the barrio and on the east side of the city. Warehouses lined the roads surrounding the railroad yard, and Donovan saw several trucks, loaded with freight bound for the next train, slowly rolling down Winchester, the main street fronting the station. He turned right as he left the station, keeping his head down and his hands in his pockets. He didn't want to draw any attention, and though it wasn't likely anyone would recognize him by day, it was always possible.

He turned down a dingy road between two warehouses, skirted a half-empty parking lot and made his way to a set of stairs leading down to what appeared to be a basement entrance on the far corner of a dingy, abandoned building. The stairs dropped away into shadows, and at the bottom, they ended at a door that had been sealed by several long planks of wood being nailed across the frame.

Donovan started down, concentrating. He closed his eyes and took three steps down, two steps back up, four down, one up, put out his hands and stepped forward. Where the boards and the door had been, solid, dirty, and cracked, a dark portal had opened. He passed through and opened his eyes. There was a loud screech in his ear, and an explosion of air. Donovan staggered forward, nearly fell to his knees, and the portal sealed behind him.

Asmodeus wheeled and soared down the corridor to his left, then executed a lazy flip and floated back to land on Donovan's shoulder with a heavy thump.

"Dark and Light, bird," Donovan said, standing upright and glaring at the old crow. "Can't you just make a normal entrance?"

The bird cocked its head to one side and watched him with sharp, intelligent eyes. Donovan sighed, turned, and took in his surroundings.

The Labyrinth ran farther than he could see in either direction. To the right, and the left, dim lights glowed in a series of alcoves. Beside each of these were doors. Some were metal, others wood. Each was unique. Donovan had walked this corridor more times than he could count, and still, he'd only touched the surface of its potential. Each door led somewhere new. Some of them even led to other times, and he suspected that if you were not careful, you might find one that led to another dimension, or even a different world.

He had been very careful in his investigations. Many of the doorways led to places close by. There were a number of doorways in San Valencez, and he knew of others in other cities. For an exploratory journey, he used great caution, anchoring himself with a series of charms he'd developed, and marking his trail through a sequence of symbols, like Ariadne's thread, used to thwart the Minotaur in Greek legend. When he was visiting a place he'd already been, he knew the pattern. Each of the doorways could lead to more than one destination. The key to coming out where you wanted to was knowing the pattern that opened that particular door. The doors opened onto crossings of the great ley lines, and if a place had enough such crossings, like San Valencez, there were many ways in and out of it. If it was a more obscure location, there might be a single door, and a single sequence of charms, that could open it.

Donovan had been to Asheville before. There was a lot of power in the mountains near the city, and he'd taken several of the more dangerous tomes in his collection from the private library at the Biltmore Mansion, back in the day. Getting to Old Mill would be a bit trickier, but again, there were a lot of lines crossing near The Great Dismal Swamp, and he suspected that the area was littered with portals. The problem was in finding the ones that best suited his purpose, and those that weren't being used by someone else. All things considered, it was entirely possible that Starkey himself was both aware of, and able to access them. That was a meeting Donovan didn't want to have in the Labyrinth. It was an ancient, powerful place, but nothing is permanent. There was no way to know what effect a significant release of energy in that tunnel might cause. It was one secret of the universe he was comfortable not knowing.

One of the anomalies of the Labyrinth, which was his own name for the series of portals, was that distance traveled while on the inside was not directly relative to point of embarkation, or destination. You could travel around the world in a few feet, if you knew the right charms, and chose the proper door. Or you could go a mile to get down the street.

He started walking, and counting, three doors on the left, two on the right. He stopped, walked backward enough paces to pass three doors and stepped forward one. Without hesitating, he turned to the doorway on his right. It was carved of stone. There was no knob, but there was a huge, horseshoe-shaped steel handle embedded in the center. He grabbed it, closed his eyes again, and spoke three words sharply. He pushed, and when he did, the stone dissolved. He stepped through and kept walking until his boot struck the bottom step of another set of stairs. He opened his eyes.

The stairway led up about ten steps to a pair of trees. The branches of those trees leaned out over the entrance, obscuring it. Donovan climbed without looking back and parted the branches, then he stopped. He stood in an open field. Around him, the ruins of a very old building gave way to moss, weather, and entropy. The stairs had led to a basement, or seemed to. The building had been a church. He sensed it immediately.

Not too far away, he saw a dirt road heading off into the woods. Actually, it must have been a driveway, of sorts, because it ended at the church. He wondered if anyone who'd worshipped there had ever owned a car, or if the ruins were from the horse and buggy days.

It didn't matter. He stepped through the trees and crossed the ruins to the road. As he started walking, he pulled out his cell phone. He glanced at it and saw that he had no signal, but a quick brush of his finger across the screen illuminated all four of the green bars. He dialed Bullfinch's number.

"Donovan," Bullfinch said, answering immediately. "Where are you?"

"Damned if I know," Donovan said. "Somewhere outside Asheville I think. I just left the ruins of a very old church, and unless I miss my guess, I'm the first one to walk this road in over a decade. I'd appreciate a ride, if you can get a fix on me?"

"Of course," Bullfinch said. "Just a second…"

A moment later, Bullfinch returned to the line.

"Keep walking. About a quarter of a mile ahead, you'll find a larger, paved road. Turn right on that and keep going. We'll have someone along to pick you up shortly."

"Thanks, Geoffrey," Donovan said. "It's beautiful out here, but I have things to do and a lot of miles to cover in a few days. Did you find anything for me?"

"I did, and I'll be happy to show it all to you once you get in here. Believe me, this is worth waiting for. You have a real problem on your hands, my friend."

"Tell me something new," Donovan said. "I have four undead problems racing across the country in a tinted glass rolling coffin, trailed by the lady I love, all ready to converge on an ancient undead alchemist who, apparently, has forgotten how ancient vampires, or even sane ones, act. I will be all ears."

He hung up then, and kept walking. Asmodeus launched into the air and paralleled his steps, circling now and then and watching the area surrounding them with beady, predatory eyes. The sun was high and bright, the trees were green, and though it was brisk, the mountain air was fresh and clear. It was a good day for a hike in the mountains. He thought, briefly, he'd have to bring Amethyst back and show it to her. Then, as his mind shifted to Old Mill, and the problem at hand, he hurried his steps, leaving the mountain, the old church, and the portal far behind.

CHAPTER ELEVEN

About a half hour after Donovan started walking, he heard the roar of an approaching engine. He stopped, duffel bag in hand, and waited as a Jeep topped the rise and pulled up alongside him. There was a tall, dark-haired woman behind the wheel, and when she saw him, she smiled.

He stepped around to the far side of the vehicle, then glanced at the sky and whistled. Asmodeus dropped like a streak of black lightning, thumped heavily onto his shoulder and nearly sent him sprawling, then glared into the Jeep. Donovan caught his balance, glared back at the bird. The driver of the Jeep laughed, leaned over, and opened the door.

"Get in, Donovan, while you're still on your feet." She met Asmodeus' gaze for a moment, and her smile broadened. "My, you have a new friend. I wonder…do you know how old he is?"

Donovan climbed in and closed the door.

"It's nice to see you too, Rebecca," he said. "It's been a long time." He turned to answer her smile with one of his own. "His name is Asmodeus, and no, I have no idea his age. He came to me under rather…odd circumstances. We're still getting to know one another.'"

"Know," Asmodeus squawked.

Rebecca smiled, but didn't laugh. She turned her attention to the road, did a quick U-turn, and headed back down the mountain.

"Well," she said, carefully, "I didn't mean to be rude. It's just that I'm pretty certain that I know your friend," she said. "If I am right, he has been around a very long time."

"What do you mean you know him?" Donovan asked, turning to stare at her. "When I found him, he was the familiar to a rogue wizard of questionable ability and little common sense. He couldn't speak at all. He does look very old, but I took this as a sign of…"

"You know better, Donovan," she said. "Asmodeus is a familiar. He's not a crow, and he doesn't age in the normal sense of the word. Like Cleo, he's known many of our kind. In fact, if you'd done any research—and this sort of lapse is not like you—you'd know."

"Know what?" Donovan said, turning to stare at the bird. "Have you been holding out on me, featherbrain?"

"Out!" the bird cawed, reaching over and tugging playfully at a lock of Donovan's long hair.

Rebecca laughed.

"This," she said, "is the sort of reunion I've come to expect from you. It's good to see you, Donovan."

She hesitated, and then continued. "It is good to see you too, Modo. It has been a very long time. I understand from your presence here that your master has passed…"

"Passed." The crows agreed.

"That is a shame," Rebecca said. "I had hoped to see him at least one more time. Still, as old as you are, that man was ancient."

Donovan sat back and stared at the road ahead.

"One of you going to tell me what you're talking about, or do I have to go back to San Valencez and look it up?"

The crow remained silent, and so did Rebecca, for a moment. Rebecca York was a strikingly attractive lady. She was taller than most women, with long, dark hair and an exotic complexion. Donovan had known her for many years, and had worked with her once or twice. She was well-versed in Egyptian and Israeli mysticism. What he admired most about her was her honesty and sensitivity toward the balance of things. They worked for a similar cause, and it had drawn them together more than once.

"I met a man named Geber a very long time ago, in Israel," she said. "He told me that his real name was Jabir. He had a raven who traveled with him, already old at the time. The Raven spoke fluent Egyptian, and some other Arabic languages, when it was of a mind to. Jabir claimed to have seen the tablets of Hermes. He sought the Philosopher's Stone, and though I do not believe he got any closer than others, he was powerful, and very, very old. The last I heard, he'd moved into Iraq to search for an ancient manuscript. I heard from him when he began that journey, but…"

"Passed," Asmodeus croaked. "Zagros."

Donovan turned again and stared at the bird.

"The Zagros mountains? There have long been rumors that there are scrolls hidden there, in a cave beneath an ancient mosque. I was not aware that anyone in recent times had attempted to search for them. The area is torn by war, and travel is difficult, even for those of power. I have heard of Geber, of course. I have several tomes penned by his hand in my archive, but…"

He turned to Asmodeus, and his face suddenly lit with a grin.

"You don't speak much English yet, do you, my friend? Is that it?"

"English," the bird said. It shook its wings and nearly fell off his shoulder, as if trying to brush something distasteful from its wings.

Donovan laughed. "That explains so much. The magician he traveled with when I met him was not very powerful. He bonded with Asmodeus, but he could never get him to talk. It was a particular point of frustration for him. For what it's worth, as dangerous as Cornwell was, no one deserved the death he met. Since you were bonded, I know you shared that pain. If only he'd studied more. If only he'd understood what an amazing, powerful ally he had."

Donovan turned away then. He was a believer in fate, though he also believed it could be manipulated. He wondered, very briefly, if Cornwell had only, in the end, been a vessel.

"So," he said. "I suppose Geoffrey clued you in on why I'm here. I hope he has something that will help, because from my own research, George Starkey would have been a formidable opponent before he died. Since he came back, he's become truly frightening."

"I know of your mission," Rebecca said. "I don't envy you. One thing I do know, and I believe you know it too, is that what he is doing goes against the very grain of the universe. He's taking the path of Icarus, and no matter how you mix the wax, it melts when it gets too close to the sun. I hope you can keep your companions out of the way of the blaze, but I think you know as well as I do that, regardless of what happens when you get to Old Mill, he can never succeed. It can't be allowed."

"That's why I'm here," Donovan said. "I need to understand exactly what I'm up against. Geoffrey knows the area, and apparently knows the man. He seemed like my best source."

Rebecca turned and glanced at Asmodeus just for a second.

"I wouldn't be too sure of that. How's your Egyptian?"

"Rusty."

"Well, Starkey is—was—an alchemist. He is old, as well, but his years were a puff of dust compared to Geber. You may have your best reference on your shoulder, if you figure out how to communicate."

"I'll keep that in mind," Donovan said. "I've spent most of the time since he came to me trying to keep Cleo from trying to remove his feathers, and him from going after her eyes. They have a tentative truce, but I can tell you that a task you do not want to set for yourself is keeping the peace in a home with two familiars."

"I'm sure they understand one another better than you think," Rebecca laughed. "Remember, Cleo is also Egyptian, and she is named for a queen. I wouldn't be surprised if she knows him, as well. You really do need to work on your relationships."

"It's not the first time I've heard that," Donovan said. "So, tell me about your zombie problem."

"I haven't really been part of it," she said. "Geoffrey brought in someone more qualified, in this case. I know you've heard of the O.C.L.T.—they are very resourceful. I'm sure we could help down in Old Mill, if you asked."

"I think I've got this one," Donovan said. "You have my interest now, though…someone here more qualified than *you* to handle restless dead? This is someone I can't wait to meet."

"He's already headed back to headquarters," she said, "but I'm sure you'll get your chance eventually. He's a man of science—a physicist. His name is Gunter Krieg, and he runs a research facility at Evergreen University. As it turns out, that fine line between magic and science that man has been walking like a tightrope since ancient times has come back to haunt him, I think. He's brilliant, and he knows things I can only begin to comprehend. It's a great story, and I'm sure Geoffrey will fill you in. I'm afraid I'm only acting as chauffer. I have been called to Italy—my flight leaves in the morning. As soon as I drop you off, I'll be on my way."

"That is a shame," Donovan said, "But I'm glad I had the chance to see you again. Also, it's good to learn something new. They say you do that every day, but I find that over the years it's become a little less frequent. I think 'Modo' and I here have a lot to talk about, once we figure out the logistics of it. I am feeling rather foolish, and that is another thing that hasn't happened for a while. You never cease to surprise me."

"You'd have figured it out eventually," she said. "But you know that too. I'm glad I could help the both of you, and I hope that he is able to be of assistance in what is coming, because, while I only have a slight ability with 'the sight,' I see great conflict and danger in your near future. I don't want to have to spend this whole trip worrying, so you let me know what happens."

"I'll do that," he said. "Amethyst is with me, as well. She and Cleo are running herd on the young undead. I need to meet with Geoffrey and be off to meet them. Babysitting is not my forté."

Rebecca laughed. "They couldn't be in better hands."

They drove on in silence then, Donovan gazing at the ancient bird on his shoulder in wonder, and Rebecca lost in her own thoughts and memories. It took nearly half an hour to reach the motel where Bullfinch had set up camp, and when they arrived, Donovan climbed out, then leaned back in to give Rebecca a hug.

"Be careful over in Italy," he said. "I know you wouldn't be going unless there's trouble."

"You too," she said. "You and Amethyst stop back through here on your way home and we'll swap stories. Maybe I'll give you a quick Egyptian lesson while we're at it."

"It's a date," Donovan said. He stepped back, and she pulled away from the curb. He turned to the motel and started in as Asmodeus took to the sky. He stopped for a second and watched as the small black figure spiraled up into the clouds. He smiled, shook his head, and went inside.

CHAPTER TWELVE

Bruno had driven straight through the first night, stopping once on the Nevada side for gas, and so Bones could try out a slot machine. He claimed never to have seen one, and managed, in the short span of half an hour, to drop twenty dollars in quarters, and Vein ordered them onward.

Kali had remained pretty calm during the drive, but the stop-over ate at her control. Vein, who was torn between wanting to enjoy the taste of freedom and the road, and watching over her on her quest, figured he'd yanked Bones away from the slots just in time to prevent her ripping out the guy's throat.

They spent the day in a safe house along US 40. When Vein woke, Kali was already up. She was pacing the room, staring at the door, and he knew they had to keep rolling. He understood some of what she was going through, but only through their bond. He'd fallen in love with Vanessa more than seventy years in the past. He'd known what she was almost from the beginning, and it hadn't mattered. He'd followed her willingly, even after learning that she was beyond him. What she offered had been his ticket out of a bad life on the street and an early death, or prison time.

Kali's rage was an entirely different thing. She'd had a life—a good life—and a future. It had been stolen from her, and on top of that she'd seen the same thing torn from her family as she was made to watch. Now she had some strength and power of her own, and she'd had time to dwell on what had been done to her. She had come to terms with her condition, and he thought, given time, would come to, if not cherish it as he did, accept and enjoy it. That could never happen until they got her past the guilt, and the need for revenge.

Vein had heard stories of blood quests before. They had never really registered like this. They had seemed just to be stories. Most of them had happened so far in the past that even the world they'd taken place in had moved on. Vein liked that term, moving on. He'd stolen it from a Stephen King novel—one of the Gunslinger series—and kept it for his own, because it was so precisely true. One world moved on, the next came to life around you, and before you knew it, things that had been normal and accepted were nothing more than late-night reruns and memories to be shared over a beer.

As they drove, he decided to break the silence, and the monotony. Either he'd get his head ripped off, or he'd bring them together, but he knew that if something didn't crack soon, they were just driving to their second death, and that wasn't in his itinerary.

"I was living on the street," he said.

Bones turned in his seat to stare, quizzically. Kali continued to stare straight ahead in silence, and Bruno drove without reacting. Vein sat back, turned to make it obvious he was talking to Kali, and continued.

"I had a few people who were good to me. There was a guy at a thrift store who used to give me clothes sometimes, and the night cook at one of the clubs downtown, the place that's Sid's now, slipped me food when he could. Mostly I got by stealing things, selling them, being a messenger for people too rich, scared, or wanted to be seen on the streets themselves. I carried groceries for old women and then pretended they turned me on, because they paid me. I tried the same thing with some of the men, but, well, I couldn't do that. I was about ninety-eight pounds and surviving on attitude.

"Then I met her. One night I came out of the back of that club, heading out to see if I could get a bed in the shelter over at the Church of New Light, and when I stepped into the alley, she was just there. You've all seen Vanessa."

He brushed a stray hair from Kali's cheek.

"You've felt her, through me. I was just a boy—a human boy—and she was the most beautiful thing I'd ever seen. Even if she'd taken me then, jumped me and left me to wake alone in the alley into the darkness and the blood, I would have loved her. I believe that with all my heart.

"And she did none of that. She talked to me. She made me feel as if I mattered. She took me for food and asked questions. I told her my entire life's story, and she listened. I remember now that she told me nothing about herself. Nothing but her name. When she left, she gave me money, and she took me to see a man she knew. He had a place with several rooms for rent. He gave me one, and she paid him. He gave me a job, too, working in his dry-cleaning shop. I took it, and for the first time in my life, I had money of my own, a bed to sleep in that had sheets and an old ratty blanket, and clothes that fit.

"She came to visit me, not every night, but often. Each time she did, she revealed a little more of herself. She took me on long walks around the city. I remember very clearly the first time she let me see her feed. It was a girl, maybe twenty. She worked as a waitress in a dance hall. They'd known one another for a long time, or it seemed that way. We went to the girl's rooms, and they gave me a glass of milk.

"While I was drinking, that girl—Charlene was her name—crawled into Vanessa's lap, pulled her hair back from her throat, and laid her head back as if she'd done the same thing a hundred times. Maybe she had. Vanessa looked at me. She looked at me the entire time she fed, from the moment she sank her fangs into Charlene's throat, until the moment she released the girl, who had swooned. She held her like that, rocking gently, and asked me to bring a glass of wine.

"That was the only moment I can remember where I considered not doing as she asked. I wanted to run. I was disgusted, and fascinated, and turned on and what I did, in the end, was everything she asked.

"When she walked me back to my room that night, she turned to me, held my face in her hands, and told me what she was. She explained that she had to feed to remain alive, and young, and beautiful. She asked me, if she promised not to hurt me, would I help her."

"I would have fed her then and there, but she didn't ask it. It was months later, and she'd introduced me to Johndrow by then. I was in awe of him. He was tall, rich, so well dressed that anyone who saw him out on the street stared and wished he'd turn, just for a second, to acknowledge them. When he and Vanessa were out together, and they took me along, it was like traveling with royalty. I thought he'd be jealous, but I came to understand over time that nothing could come between the two of them. I'd heard of love, but the blood bond is more intimate. More complete. I know that now, but then I thought that Vanessa spending time with me might anger him."

"You seem a little too old for that story," Bones commented, cutting in. "How old were you when you were on the street?"

"Seventeen," Vein said. "It was nearly eight years before I went to Vanessa, and to Johndrow, and formally requested my transformation. They never suggested it, or offered it. It was always there between us, though. I believe, if I'd never said anything, I would have grown older, become less attractive to them, and that they would have set me up for a successful life and gone on their way. Eventually I couldn't stand it. I wanted what they had and they offered it freely."

"Why are you telling us this?" Kali asked, turning to him. "You know my story. All of you do. You shared it, and you know that this means nothing to me. I can't even imagine a world where the one who turned me was someone to be admired. I have thought of very little but his final death since the moment I escaped."

"I know," Vein said softly. "I know, and yes, I have shared. I wanted you to know that he isn't all of it. I wanted you to know that, when this is over, you aren't alone. You aren't out on the street, or lonely, or stuck in some eternal void. You have me. You have all of us, and you have a world to discover, and enjoy. There are rules, we abide by them. This… Starkey…does not. I will face final death to ensure we avenge the deaths of your family, and the theft of your humanity. We are bound. What I want to feel, what I want to know that you feel, is that when that is accomplished, you still have a family. You still have a life, a different sort of life, to live."

The silence held for a few minutes longer, and then Kali spoke.

"I know that," she said. "God, I know what you are all risking for me. I even know that what we're doing is stupid and potentially suicidal. I'm not stupid. I can't help it. It's like someone put a pipe through my skin and started pumping in anger. If I spend very long at a time being still, I think about him. I think about my mother, and my brother, my father, my town. How many more has he killed? How many did he take before me? There are a lot of drug dealers, homeless people, and poor people around Old Mill. No one would have noticed. When I think about that, I realize that I wouldn't have noticed either, and I get angrier. If I don't kill him, if I don't do something to erase him and be certain that what he has done, and what he *is* doing has come to an end, I'll go crazy. You won't know me. I'll go out one night and kill and kill and kill until something takes me out and removes the pain."

"We're going to get him," Bones said. "I'll promise to throw myself on him and sacrifice myself, if you please, please don't make me tell my own boring story, because as much fun as this all is, I spent my time in group therapy, and it did me no good at all."

They laughed at this, and the sound was welcome. It broke the tension like a hammer on brittle ice.

"It's two hundred miles to Memphis," Bruno cut in. "If we're done with our love fest, we have to make a decision. There are five separate safe houses in range. Most of them are on the outskirts of town, one is just off Beale. I'll have to make a choice soon."

Vein stared out the window for a moment, then turned to watch Kali as he spoke.

"I have never been to Beale Street. Elvis walked there, and sang there, and chased women and took too many drugs there. I want to feel that. Since this may be the last trip we ever take, what say we take a short detour. It's a long way from San Valencez, and I'm hungry for something fresher than a bag of A+ from a local clinic. One night—to see Memphis. We spend tomorrow in the safe house, have our night, return to the safe house, and it's off to Old Mill, North Carolina at nightfall."

Kali sat very still. She wanted to tell him to go on. She wanted to say no, but these three were about to risk their very existence for her. One night. She'd lived with her rage a very long time. What could one more night hurt?

"One night," she said. She nodded. "One night—for you."

Vein pulled her close then and Bruno stepped on the gas. A little while later they saw the faint glow of Memphis break the skyline.

"This," Bones said, "is going to be epic."

CHAPTER THIRTEEN

When Vein woke, he found Kali already up, pacing the room and stopping, now and again, to stare out through the east facing wall of the safe house into some unseen distance. He watched her for a few moments, taken by her grace, the fluidity of her motion, and the intensity of her hatred. She was beautiful, powerful, and magnificent, he thought. She prowled like a caged beast.

He rose and she turned.

"I want to *go*," she said.

"I know you do, love," he said, "and we will. I think we owe it to these knuckleheads to give them a last fling, though, don't you? Especially considering that, regardless of how this all comes out, it's likely to be *the* last fling for one or more of us. Besides, aren't you hungry? I mean, sure, we have what we packed, but, I don't know, after a while plastic-bagged blood just doesn't seem to cut it for me. If we were home we could hit the club, find someone willing, but here? I have no idea what to expect, but I expect to feed."

"It's dangerous," Kali said evenly. "If we cross some line that we don't even know is there, we might bring down the Memphis version of the High Council on our heads. Worse still, what if we wander into someone's hunting ground? I don't like it. I think we should get in the car and push on."

Around them, the others had awakened and stood silently, waiting.

"We're staying here tonight," Vein said firmly. "We're going out to see this town, hear some music, find some blood with a little wine in it, and enjoy ourselves. Tomorrow we'll be back on the blood quest as if we never stopped, stronger and refreshed."

Kali didn't reply. She turned away. He walked up to her and put his hands on her shoulders. She flinched, but then a moment later she melted back against him. The others relaxed. They sided with Vein, as always, but they knew Kali. She was dangerous, and they would not cross her given another option. But none of them wanted to miss this night on the town.

The safe house was about five blocks from Beale Street. It was already dark out, and the evening's festivities were well underway. They could hear the hum of sound from the various clubs on the main drag, as well as the flow of traffic and the cries and laughter of people on the streets. It was Friday, and the weekend had begun. Vein and the others stood for a while on the street, taking in the scents and sounds of the city, before moving ahead.

"Still dinner time," Vein said. "The clubs will be open, but not packed yet. I say we start at one end and work our way down. We can hit the shops, catch a couple of the early bands, and see what's what. If we're lucky, we'll find something that suits us before the crowds really kick in, and we can circle back. We're in a new place, so we'll have to be practical. Check for rear doors. Check for alleys. We need a club with a lot of people, loud music, and quick access to the streets."

"Christ," Bones said, "are we going for a night on the town or a military raid? Can't we just go with the flow and see where it takes us?"

"We can, and we will," Vein said, "but just because you're all big and bad and powerful doesn't mean you can't be taken down. You'd do well to remember that, particularly considering the situation we're heading into. It's not going to make much of a story when we get back if we don't even get past Memphis."

Bones rolled his eyes, but kept his silence. Bruno, as usual, said nothing. He walked a step behind them and closer to the street, looking for all the world like their older uncle watching over them as they took to the streets.

Neon winked and blinked, sending up a brightly colored glow that gleamed in rainbow halos around the tops of the clubs, shops, restaurants and other establishments. Most of it was glitz and glitter aimed at tourists, but if you looked closely, you could see through the cheap makeup and eyeliner. It was an old city, not in the sense of the cities of the Old World, but ancient in relation to the new. Myths and legends had walked those streets. Powers had played, won, lost and loved in the clubs and bars and alleys. Something of that remained, and that was what Vein was after.

He looked for the same thing in San Valencez, every time he went out. He looked for the world he remembered as a child. He looked for the world

Vanessa knew as a child, or Johndrow. He wanted to peel away the layers and bring back what was old and majestic and powerful, and it was always just out of reach.

On Beale Street, it suddenly felt closer again. There were a few places, like "Mr. Handy's Blues Hall," that preserved the ancient like a shrine. Vein liked the blues. He liked music, in general. This place echoed with music that had been played so many years in the past it was etched into the stone walls and the paved sidewalks. The dirt was dirt that Robert Johnson might have crossed, and every corner they turned brought them another piece of the past, albeit covered or broken or changed.

"This is what I'm talking about," Vein said. "This is the kind of town where you can live. Where you can't help it. This is just a regular Friday night. It's still early, and look at this place. It's like San Valencez's naughty little sister."

"More like a two-dollar hooker," Bones said. "This place is all about money, and fleecing tourists. I wonder how long it's been since it was real?"

"Oh, it's still real," Vein said. "Trust me. This is the main drag, and even here, you can feel it. Let's do our tourist thing and make it quick. Then I think we'd better hit some of the side streets, zig zag through the less glamorous side of the city, and find something old. Something that matters."

"You are one weird dude," Bones said, laughing. "Onward then. What the hell. I'm thirsty, and I can hear music from here that isn't half bad."

They walked. They slipped in and out of clubs. They chatted up locals and tourists alike, listened to some blues, and all the while Vein kept his eye on the side streets. There were dimmer lights, and darker alleys to be had, and he knew if their hunt was going to be successful they were going to have to leave Beale behind eventually. He just wanted to make sure that whatever dive they ended up in had music, and style. The others thought they were just wandering, but Vein had decided. He was going to find and taste something that was truly a part of this place. He wanted it to be a part of him.

Finally they turned down a narrow alley and followed it for several blocks. When they came out on the far side, a single set of blue and green lights glimmered across the way. A battered wooden sign above the door read, "Something Blue."

"My friends," Vein said, stopping to stare at the old sign, "I believe that we've arrived."

The air pulsed with a syncopated backbeat that carried to their ears. The guitar was too soft to make out at such a distance, but the drums and the bass teased at their skin. Vein started walking, and the others followed. They did not look both ways when they crossed the street, as they'd been taught as children, and they failed to be careful, as Vein had promised. They heard the music, and they followed it.

In the shadows at the end of the alleyway they'd exited, a tall, almost cadaverous figure watched them in silence. He wore a very long black jacket that swept the ground, despite the warmth in the air. He wore a battered fedora pushed down in front so that it covered his eyes. He wore an old dreadnaught guitar slung across his shoulders, and silver buckles gleamed on the sides of scuffed, black boots. He leaned on the wall of the alley, stared at the entrance to "Something Blue." He pulled out a small pouch and a pack of rolling papers. Very slowly, he rolled a smoke, tucked it between his lips, and returned the papers and tobacco to his pocket. He breathed in, and the cigarette lit, the bright end like a sizzling spark as it caught. There was no lighter or match.

There was a regular crowd that attended the club. There were a few underground bands who turned up now and again that drew them. There was whiskey and beer. The air in the club was permeated with the blues, the scent of the city, and the taste of the past. It was a very old club, older than most of those on Beale and a lot more authentic.

The stranger lifted his hat brim. Pale, luminous globes glimmered where his eyes should have been. He cocked his head, and he listened. He felt their footsteps as they prowled the bar. He heard their words, their laughter, their predatory breath as they moved between the patrons of "Something Blue" like a pack of wild animals on the hunt.

It was a quiet club. Sometimes, when there were only a few old men sipping their whiskey and forgetting the sadness of wasted lives, he went inside, and he played. He'd played on that small stage for a hundred years, and before that, he'd played others. He'd walked the country roads of the South and fought his way through the juke joints and spit-hole dives. He always came back. "Something Blue" was his home, his nest, and it drew him like the family he could barely remember and the words to the old songs that sometimes slipped in and out of his mind, shifting and changing with the breeze.

These others, they didn't belong. The beat of their boots on the floor of the club was out of sync with the music. The heat in their eyes, and the chill in their veins smelled of salt water, not the delta. He felt their hunger, and he knew he had to quench it. Permanently. He couldn't allow them to walk away with something that was his. He'd been watching the club for a very long time. He was the only one that ever walked away.

Blind Johnny Jones slid the guitar off his shoulder, slung it low, and brushed his cracked nails over the strings. The strings were silver and bright and the pale moonlight that caught their motion quivered and sparkled. His fingers walked up the neck, and he picked a 12 bar blues pattern, sliding and bending notes to fit the song to the night. He'd been wrong before—he had to be sure. He played and then, before the notes could fade to silence, he dipped his hand into his pocket, pulled it free and dropped a handful of white animal bones to the dirt at his feet.

They formed patterns. He knelt, reached down and brushed his fingers over the alley floor, found the bones and traced their lines. He lingered on each, testing the lay and the angle, piecing the image together in his mind. Then he snapped them up neatly and dropped them back into his pocket.

Something dark and wet remained in the dirt. He dipped his fingertip into it, and traced an equal-armed cross on each of his cheeks. He dipped again, and drew a symbol in the white center of his forehead, between his sightless eyes.

Then he rose, and, circling slowly, he made his way around to the rear of "Something Blue," sliding the guitar back over his shoulder and keeping carefully to the shadows, where he blended in like the slat-silhouette of a picket fence, or a particularly tall, thin insect. He knew they would exit from the rear. Their kind always did, slinking back into the shadows. That was where he would wait for them. That was where they would die a second and final time. Then, Johnny thought, he would play—maybe until the sun rose and he shimmered out of sight. Maybe this time it would be the last show, and he'd play in the morning sun.

Maybe not. It was a very dark night.

CHAPTER FOURTEEN

The private car Donovan had arranged was luxurious, and the steady rattle and sway of the train was surprisingly relaxing. Amethyst sat at the small table in the room with several bookmarked volumes stacked beside her, and a leather journal open. She had a cup of hot tea, and on the short bench across from her, staring up at her with curious yellow eyes, Cleo lent moral support.

The big cat had been out of her carrier since the moment the door to the cabin had been closed, and after prowling the interior and inspecting every inch of horizontal space, she'd claimed the wide seat on one side of the table as her own and stretched out for the ride.

The work was slow going. Amethyst's specialty was charms, crystals, and amulets. While these were great for protection, it was much more difficult to plan for direct conflict. She had an arsenal of weapons at her disposal, but they were generally narrowly focused. It magnified the problem that her allies and her enemy were all undead.

The sun crystals she'd used to good effect against Vein and his friends in the past would probably work to some extent on the ancient vampire as well, but they would have the side-effect of incapacitating her companions. She needed to be able to participate in the coming confrontation, if the need arose, without doing more harm than good.

The alchemy angle was disturbing as well. As an alchemist, and a very old, talented one at that, Starkey would know the rudiments of her craft—possibly more. He had no reason to expect an attack, but that didn't mean he hadn't been smart enough to take precautions. She held the journal open with one hand and leaned down to rummage through her leather carry-on bag. She'd packed a wide variety of supplies, charms, equipment and the bits and pieces she needed to make more. The train trip was providing her the time to get it right; she took full advantage.

The first thing she'd worked on was a wand. She always smiled when she thought about wands. Magic wands were such a cliché magician's prop. What she'd created was something different entirely. She'd found the design in a very old book Donovan had loaned her. It was a maple rod tipped with one of the sun crystals. Around the tip, mounted on a frame that pointed their tips inward toward the central crystal, like the legs of an odd spider, were darker crystals. Each of them had been carefully prepared, as had the tip—the one to soak in the power of the sun, the others to bend and focus it into a narrow beam.

As with most magical weapons, if she aimed it at a man, or a woman, the worst they might get was momentary blindness, or a slight sunburn. The purpose of the weapon was to kill the undead, and for that purpose it was precise, and deadly. It could be aimed, the beam directed in a very tight blast.

She'd also worked out some shields, for herself and Donovan. She had others they could offer to Kali and her friends, but that was a worst-case scenario. Best case, the two of them stood by and watched so they could report back that everyone was safe. In theory, with what Donovan had explained to them, and what Kali already knew, the young undead should have a fighting chance of taking Starkey down on their own. It was important to Kali that she be the instrument of destruction, and that made helping more difficult.

It didn't mean she, or Donovan, needed to put themselves at extra risk. She didn't know what Donovan had planned, and that was frustrating as well. She worked quickly, threading crystals onto a series of long, thread-thin wires. What she was creating was a shield that Donovan would be familiar with. She had made one, and he had it, but she needed one of her own. The crystals threaded onto the wire were green and clear. The wires met in the center, where there was a handle that one could slip their fingers into. If you whirled your wrist just right, the blurring crystals formed a shield impervious to just about anything, magical or physical, but only in a direct line—like the shields of ancient warriors.

It was busy work. She had other charms that would work as well, but she needed to keep busy, and she'd done all the delving in ancient manuscripts her mind could take for one night. She glanced over at Cleo.

"He owes us big, you know. I hate homework, and the one thing I hate even more is babysitting. You think maybe we should check in on our 'charges'?"

The train would pull into Memphis in less than an hour. It was one of the last places she could get off before moving on to North Carolina. The train was an express, and there were few stops.

She tied off the last of the threads, tested the knots on each to be sure that the crystals were secure, and packed it away with the rest of her materials. Then she pulled out a small metal stand, and a single, flawless crystal sphere. She also pulled out a carefully rolled square of black silk. She unrolled this on the table and placed the stand on the center. The cloth was carefully embroidered with magical circles, much like the ones Donovan went to such pains to draw each time. Amethyst wasn't any less careful than he was, but she knew the boundaries of what she needed very clearly. To use the crystal for seeing, she did not need the full protection of a circle—it was more of a precaution. She placed the four braziers, lit very small cones of incense in each, and whispered the invocations, one to each cardinal point of the circle.

Almost immediately, the wispy smoke from the small braziers whirled into a cylinder of mist around the outside of the crystal. Amethyst closed her eyes. She pictured Vein in her mind, building the image carefully from bits and pieces of memory. She used the weak blood bond to strengthen the connection. When she had the image as clear as possible, she opened her eyes and whispered "*Wys my*" and blew directly into the whirling mist. It cleared, and the crystal took on an odd shimmer. She stared into its depths, as if she might impose her own image of Vein into that tiny, spherical window.

First, she saw colored lights. There was no sound, but she sensed it. She concentrated, and the lights clarified into a sign. "Something Blue." She concentrated harder. Something felt wrong. She sensed Vein's presence, and could see that it was a club he was in—not smart considering their mission, and how far away they were from home—but still, just a club.

A shadow shifted to one side of the crystal. Amethyst ground her teeth. She couldn't glance over to see what it was. If she tried, she'd have to remove her concentration from Vein, and she might lose the image entirely. Whatever was there was very dark. She calmed herself, took a deep breath, and willed her peripheral vision to expand. She knew that if she got in a hurry, or became frustrated, the image would fade and she might not be able to get it back. There was also the danger to which she would alert Vein that he was being watched. The blood bond was too new for her to trust.

The image broadened. She saw the street, and could make out the buildings to either side of the club. The shadow took shape slowly. It was a man, very tall, and very thin. He was smoking, and he had something slung across his back. He was watching the club with cool patience, and the darkness around him pulsed unnaturally. She sensed no heat, no life, and yet there was power.

Then, everything changed. The figure turned and stepped forward. She found herself face to face with a set of milky-white, sightless eyes that seemed to bore into her soul. She felt a power slipping in through her crystal, reaching for the edges or the circle as if to test them.

She closed her eyes and snapped out a single word. "Einde!" The mist dissipated. The energy that had crackled in the air was simply gone. Amethyst shook her head to clear the cobwebs of that other mind from her own and opened her eyes. Cleo stood up, back arched and hair on end, glaring at the crystal.

"It's okay girl," she said. "He's not there anymore. I don't think we're going to be riding through to North Carolina though. Whoever that is, he's not friendly, and I'm afraid he's hunting our little hunters."

She rose, packed her things, and then moved to the small window on the side of the car, watching as they pulled into the outer limits of the Memphis train yards.

"We'd better call Donovan too, don't you think, Cleo?" she said, turning back. Cleo didn't answer. Instead, she washed her front paw, watching the now dormant crystal ball with studied distrust.

"Why can't it ever be simple?" Amethyst said softly. "Donovan, you owe me *big!*"

CHAPTER FIFTEEN

"So," Donovan said, sitting back and staring at the book propped on his knee, "Starkey has been in North Carolina most of his undead life."

"From what I've been able to unearth," Bullfinch said, "He never really gave up his studies. It seems that he had all the equipment stashed that he believed he might need, possibly even a fully equipped laboratory located deep in the swamp that he provided for before leaving for Europe. It was kind of ironic. He went there searching for vampires, and he walked into the mouth of The Black Plague. He was lucky not to have died, as has always been believed, in that debacle. Possibly he was ill, or beginning to feel the effects of plague, when he found what he was after."

"No vampire that I've ever met would feed on someone dying of the plague," Donovan said, closing the book slowly. "They would have smelled it on him and left him to die."

"I know," Bullfinch said. "That's why I dug deeper. There is a legend in Wales, not a legend we'd run across in our lore, because it's told by the undead to their peers. It's the story of a sorcery—long dead to the world—that allowed a mage to compel a vampire to feed. It was a charm that rendered a man's blood irresistible, and then, once consumed, compelled the undead to bring that mortal back. It wasn't a permanent spell, but once cast, the damage was done. No one has ever located a copy of the formula, but it is said that one accomplished it, and then, he disappeared."

"To America," Donovan finished.

"It certainly fits," Bullfinch agreed. "There's more, of course. He can never return to Europe. As you know, all true legends have their roots in fact. There is an ancient in London. He's been chained for centuries, locked away by his people. He's absolutely mad—unable to control his hunger, bent, and ugly. It's the effect of Bubonic Plague on his undead metabolism. They pretend that they don't know who caused it, but if it were not for the ocean standing between, they'd have come for him."

"That's another thing," Donovan said. "The crossing. So few have ever made it successfully, and those were ancient and powerful, with the aid of magic. Starkey would have been newly dead, weak in the blood, and probably still weak himself from the plague. How could he have returned? How could he survive?"

"These are the questions that should concern you the most," Bullfinch said, "and it's also one of the things I'm not going to be much help with, I'm afraid. He should not have been able to do it. The only explanation is that he was very powerful, and very precise. He would have had to have researched spells, charms, anything to keep him alive in the hold of a ship, and he'd have had to have help. Someone sealed him in, and someone removed that coffin filled with dirt. Someone who knew what he planned, and when he returned, what he was, and let him go anyway."

"My god," Donovan said softly. "He's not alone."

"Well, he wasn't at some point, old boy," Bullfinch agreed. "It's just not possible to have pulled it off on his own."

"It's strange," Donovan said. "I mean, the story makes sense, the timeline is right, but how did he keep all of this secret once he returned? Why are there no legends here? Where are the grimoires? Not a record, or even a rumor, in all these years? The High Council in San Valencez *shared* with that girl, Geoffrey. They felt him directly, and that means, if they had any idea he existed, they should know, or at least suspect, what they encountered. All they took away from it was that he was ancient, powerful, and not acting like an ancient, powerful vampire."

"We're dealing with a creature clever beyond anything we've encountered, my friend," Bullfinch said. "He must have fed in secret. Perhaps others hunted for him, and if he had the ability to compel an ancient vampire when he was alive, how powerful would his control have been over young vampires once he'd risen? And what might he have promised them."

"What do you mean?" Donovan asked.

"Well, you told me yourself," Bullfinch said, reaching for his pipe and tobacco. "He's trying to walk around in the bloody daylight, isn't he? Maybe he promised to bring them with him. Then, when he was old enough, and powerful enough, if they became a risk, he killed them."

"Or maybe," Donovan said thoughtfully, "they were willing guinea pigs. Maybe he experimented on them as he tried to perfect his process? An alchemy of blood—the new philosopher's stone."

"Brings more questions than answers," Bullfinch said. He filled the pipe, tamped it down, and lit it. "Why is he active again now? He's reached an age where his kind should be able to rely on fewer and fewer feedings. Many at that age are dormant, or considering it. Instead, he's acting more and more like a young one—out of character for both the man he was, and the vampire he is. Why?"

"If he's powered up," Donovan said, "I mean, he's managing to fight off the effects of the sun for several hours a day, maybe it has a cost. Maybe he has to feed more often, or in greater quantity."

"Or perhaps," Bullfinch mused, "It's a symptom of simple human frailty. He has been a vampire for a very long time, but before that, he was a man. He may have been able to stave off the effects through ritual or magical shields, but when he died, he was already dying. He had the plague. If it's been eating at his mind for centuries, maybe he's losing the ability to work. Maybe the concentration and the memories, are flaking away. That ancient vampire in Europe was very powerful. The plague blood drove him mad."

"A lot to think about," Donovan said. "Also puts what's to come in new perspective. If he's lost his hunters—his lab rats—and I have to think that's what he had in mind for Kali, as well, then sending a troupe of young vamps in to destroy him might be exactly what he's hoping for. Either he's as mad as you say, and we've got a crazy, ancient vampire on our hands, or something much worse."

"Agreed," Bullfinch said. "If he took her, turned her, tortured her family in front of her, and then let her go, he must be hoping that they will come for him. He's building a new crew to finish the work."

"Yes, and worse still," Donovan said, "she thinks she knows something that will hurt him. Whatever she did to escape, she thinks it worked. She may be counting on it as some sort of edge, or secret weapon."

"While Starkey," Bullfinch said, "sees her as nothing but bait."

At that moment, the sound of a temple chime interrupted their conversation. Donovan glanced down, then reached into one of the many pockets of his long, dark jacket and pulled out his phone. He glanced at it, answered, and put it to his ear.

"Amethyst. It's good to hear from you. I trust the children are well?"

"Not now, Donovan," she said hurriedly. "We've got trouble, and I think it's big."

"What? Where are you?"

She filled him in quickly. Then she described the creature that had tried to reach back to her through the crystal. Donovan listened carefully.

"Don't do anything," he said. "Promise me. I need to check a couple of things, and then I'm coming to join you. This might be worse, even more than you think."

"Hurry, then," she said. "Vein and the others are in that club for the moment, but unless I'm missing my guess, they'll be slipping out to escort their dinner home soon. If whatever that thing is gets to them before you get here, I'm going to have a fight on my hands, and I'm not even sure what kind."

"Stall if you can," Donovan said. "If it comes down to it, cause a diversion, anything to buy some time. I will be there as soon as possible."

He hung up without waiting for a reply and tersely told Bullfinch what he'd just heard.

"Not good," Bullfinch said. "It's Blind Johnny, has to be. The eyes, the guitar. He's bound to those streets by the music. I'd have thought he might have faded by now, but…"

"Nothing ever fades completely," Donovan said. "What do you suggest?"

"He's a thing of the crossroads," Bullfinch said. "He's not a demon—he was a musician in his day. He believes he's doing good. He's protecting the music, and the streets, and he's got power."

Bullfinch laid his pipe aside, rose, and crossed the room to his bags.

"Lucky for you, I came prepared for my own little outing. The South is littered with things powered by one sort of cross, or another. He dug through one of his bags, drew out a leather pouch, turned, and walked back to the table. He set it in front of Donovan. "Dust from a crossroad," he said. "Gathered by the light of the full moon."

Donovan lifted the bag carefully, hefted it for a moment, and then it disappeared into his jacket.

"One day," Bullfinch said, "you're going to have to show me what all you carry in those pockets, and how it's stored. I swear I have sat up nights thinking about it, and it eludes me."

Donovan rose and smiled.

"If we get through all of this alive," he said, "I'll come and visit and explain anything you'd like to hear. I'm going to need a ride."

"Absolutely," Bullfinch said. "Let me get my jacket."

They left then, and Bullfinch drove with surprising speed and ability through the shadowed back roads to the ruins of the old church. Donovan stepped out, and Asmodeus, who'd taken to the air the minute they'd left the motel, dropped onto his shoulder with a *thunk*.

"Be well, old friend," Bullfinch said. "I'd still like to talk to you about what we're doing at the O. C. L. T. I know you're not a joiner, but..."

"We'll talk," Donovan said. They shook hands, and he turned away quickly. "For now, though, duty, and a very hot redhead, call."

"I'll eagerly await the story, when you're in a position to tell it," Bullfinch said. "I'll bring the wine."

Donovan smiled, waved, and stepped through the ruins toward the old stone steps. A moment later there was a soft shimmer, and he was gone.

CHAPTER SIXTEEN

The club was very dark. It didn't matter to Vein, or the others, but it was darker than the clubs of San Valencez. It was also larger than it had seemed from the outside. It might once have been some sort of small warehouse or store. The main floor had round, wooden tables around the edge. There was a small stage against the right-hand wall, not big enough for more than a small combo. Speakers were stacked to either side that looked like something from a 1960s band documentary. The floor was hardwood, unpolished, and old.

The bar ran along the wall across the club from the stage. Rows of goblets and tumblers lined shelves and hung from a framework above the counter. The back wall was mirrored, and in front of the mirror, more bottles stood like soldiers awaiting battle. They were arranged by color, and type, age and price. Vein inspected them, and smiled.

"Johndrow would love this place," he said. Then he fell silent, surprised at the thought—both that it was of someone else, and that it was Johndrow that came to mind, and not Vanessa. Things were changing.

Though it was early, there was a crowd. They were young and well dressed—a sort of artsy group. Vein and the others fit in well enough. Their California leather look was a little off to the left of the norm, but not far enough to draw more than passing interest. The crowd wasn't there to focus on newcomers, or even, it seemed, to party or make quick pickups. The conversations were low-key. Most of those present were gathered in groups, and there was an air of expectancy permeating the place.

"It's weird," Bones said. "Like being in the crowd at a concert before the band shows up."

"Yeah," Vein said, leaning on the bar to get a better view of the crowd, "but where's the band?"

The bartender stepped up behind him, and Vein turned.

"What'll you have," the man asked. He wore a white button-down shirt, open about halfway down to show a gold chain with a dangling pendant. His hair was slicked back, longish, and he had a beard that he could have forked if he'd felt the urge. His eyes were slate gray and appraising.

Vein smiled.

"I'll have whatever red wine you have a lot of," he said. "The same for my lady. I'm guessing the other two will have beer."

He glanced at Bones, who shrugged and nodded, and Bruno who actually, for the first time on the entire trip, smiled.

"Beer it is," the bartender said. "The wine I'll have to charge for the bottle, if that's okay? We don't get a lot of call for it, and I hate to pop a cork and let it die."

"Sounds good," Vein said.

The drinks appeared quickly. The club was filling up rapidly, and the bartender, working alone, was a little harried.

"What's happening here tonight?" Vein asked, taking the bottle and two glasses. "Why is everyone so keyed up?"

"You didn't know?" the bartender said. He grinned. "You must be the luckiest tourists on the planet. It's the band…or, really, just the man. Sweet Sammy Silver's playing tonight. Blues—guitar, harp, one of the best, and oldest, in the business. He doesn't play in public much these days."

"Thanks," Vein said. "Sounds like we did get lucky."

He turned back and glanced at the stage speculatively. He had no idea who or what Sweet Sammy might be, but the room was filling quickly with hot, pulsing veins. The scent of fresh blood washed over and through him; he closed his eyes and grinned.

He led the others to one of the last empty tables, far in the back, and sat down. He poured the wine, handed one glass to Kali, and held his up for a toast. Bones slid in beside him, and Bruno took the seat on the far side, his back to the wall, watching the room. The big man wasn't as trusting as Vein. He sipped his beer, and his smile was genuine, but he wasn't about to be taken by surprise in a strange place. Vein watched him for a second, smiled, and the smile widened when, grudgingly, Kali clinked her glass against his.

"It smells wonderful," Vein said. "If the music is half as good as the crowd," he took a sip, "and the wine, we are in for a night never to be forgotten."

"It's weird," Bones said again. "I thought we'd be in, have a couple of drinks, find some willing donors, and head back…but this? It doesn't strike you odd that we came to this place, this night, when some special blues man who never plays in public shows up?"

"You're being paranoid," Vein said. "It's one of your better traits. Yes, it's odd. This time, though, I think we either decide it's fate, and we have no control over it, or it's coincidence—which I'm led to believe doesn't exist. Either way, we're here. Shall we play it out, or turn and run like children?"

Bones glared at him for a second, and then broke into a toothy grin.

"Once more into the breach, and all that," he said. He raised his beer, took a drink, and tipped it toward Vein.

"That's the spirit," Vein said.

Then the room grew very silent, and they all turned toward the stage.

Vein was surprised. It set his nerves on edge and his senses on guard. He was not often surprised, and it was not a sensation that appealed to him. The band, such as it was, was simply there. One moment the stage was bare, and the next, a very old man with very dark skin and eyes that were absolutely black sat on the stool behind the central microphone. He held a guitar so old that its finish had gone hazy, no longer smooth or glossy. His hair was gray and hung about his shoulders in uncombed disarray. Behind him, a man with a dark bandanna tied around his head, wearing totally unnecessary sunglasses, sat behind a simple drum kit. Beside the guitarist, an even older man stood, a blues-harp held loose and easy in one hand. When he smiled, a gold tooth glittered.

"This seem right to you?" Bones whispered.

Vein shrugged. His eyes never left the guitarist. "It's an interesting act," he said. "What can we do now but wait and see? Run? Hide in our safe house and talk about how much fun we might have had if we'd just sat still, enjoyed our drinks, and listened?"

"Go to hell," Bones said. He turned back to the stage.

Vein saw that the others were captivated. Something was working here, something more than just a simple performance. Those gathered knew it. He sensed nothing otherworldly in any of them. He sensed no one of the blood. It was not like Club Chaos back in San Valencez, where the crowd might have been a blend of undead, magicians, and any number of supernatural creatures, he did not believe this place was the same. There was too much blood—hot, pulsing blood. It was something else.

"It's the place," Bruno said.

They turned to him. He shrugged.

"It's this place. This club. It's old. I've been in places like this before. There's magic in that man on the stage, but if he were out on the street? Just an old man with a guitar. It's the history here that makes it magic.'"

"Where did you learn *that*?" Vein asked, still staring.

"I read," Bruno said evenly. "I talk less than the rest of you. It gives me time."

Vein met Bruno's glare for a moment. Then, unable to hold back the mirth, the edges of his mouth twitched into a smile, and then, despite the angry mutters and glares it brought from the rest of the crowd in the club, he laughed.

"You surprise me, my friend," he said. "That's twice tonight—once when they appeared on stage, and now. So…we are in a magic place are we? A place of power? Then the music should be amazing, the drinks should be more potent than normal, and the hunt…the hunt should be unforgettable."

Just then, a single chord rippled through the room. The amplifier was old, tube-powered and clear. Every voice in the room, including Vein's, grew silent. There was a susurrant shimmer as the drummer rattled his sticks over the snare light as the whisper of silk.

In the moment of silence that followed, the harp player blew one high, clean note, then rippled it down through a scale that was pure, fast, and powerful. By the time he hit the scale's bottom end, the guitar was there—a slow, sultry walk through a twelve bar progression. It was old-school, gritty and filled with emotion—so charged from the start that even without the vocals the song painted images of desolation, despair—loneliness and unrequited love.

Then the old man began to sing.

Vein knew a lot about the blues. He'd had time, decades longer than most, to study it, learn it, and familiarize himself with it. It was a music that appealed to him, often sounding the same, song to song, to untrained ear, yet always different. He'd never heard this song. He was pretty sure that even the progression was unique, and that was so unlikely that his natural arrogance and surety were, at least momentarily, stilled.

"The road is dark, so dark,
Black whiskey drowned the light.
The road is dark, so…very dark,

The whiskey took away my light.
Now I walk the hills in search of,
Something just beyond my sight…"

They sat in silence, watching and listening, as the old musician played, and sang. His emotions leaked out with the words, and the notes. They quivered on the strings of the guitar and rode the brighter, clearer notes of the harp up through the hazy, smoky air. Vein thought, momentarily, that it was odd there was smoke. Almost nowhere in California you could smoke in a club. He doubted it was any more common here, regardless of tradition.

The others were as captivated as he was, and again, it gave him pause. It wasn't natural. They'd come here to hunt. They'd come to find and seduce some young people with plenty of hot, red blood to spare, convince them to share it, have a memorable night on the town, and then get back onto the road. It had already become something more, and he wasn't sure how to read it. He knew, regardless of what happened, that he was the De Facto leader—the oldest, probably the smartest, though Bones and Kali might both contest it. He'd grown some over the past year, he knew that as well, and he felt the responsibility he'd so long ignored. If he wasn't the smartest, he was a bit wiser, and in the world at large, that was probably more important.

And yet, here they sat, hundreds of miles from home, on unknown turf, in a bar where the music appeared to have a magical quality of its own and the club felt as if it had drifted back through time. Wiser or not, he was still too impulsive. The night had only just begun, and he was already worrying over how he'd get them safely back undercover, and on the road.

"I feel the blood, pourin' through my veins,
It's movin' slower, takin' its time,
Like travelin' the rail on the dead men's trains,
I'm moving so much slower, just takin' my time…"

Vein leaned back and listened, but he didn't let the music move him as fully as it had in those first few seconds. Something was going on. It might be one of the coolest experiences of his long life, or a threat of being the last. Whichever way it went, he wanted to be ready for it.

CHAPTER SEVENTEEN

In the alley out back of "Something Blue," Blind Johnny Jones sat on an old wooden packing crate pressed up against the brick wall of a warehouse. The guitar rested on his knee, and his fingers danced over the silver-toned strings. His gaze was directed at the rear exit of the club, and anyone who'd caught his shadow, kicked back in the darkness, might have thought he was watching something very carefully. Johnny hadn't watched anything in a century. Not in the normal sense.

He felt things. He sensed energies and patterns. Most of the time, he felt nothing. His world was one of almost perpetual darkness. When he was called—when he walked the streets—he played. He watched. He protected. He heard the music floating out from the club, and though the skin was stretched tightly over his teeth and lips, he cracked a bony smile.

It was good. It wasn't quite what he'd known in the day, but he felt the connection, and his own picking wound into the pattern. He dipped his head and concentrated. The dark children he'd followed through the alley were inside, but they were quiet. He felt nothing from them and so, he gave himself to the music.

There was something else, he knew, something bright and glittering and near. He felt another presence, and there was power in it, but he did not feel a particular threat. With the strings dancing under his fingers, and more power suffusing the night air than he could remember, Blind Johnny sat tight, and he played. He willed his own notes in through the back wall of the club and joined his *mojo* with the dark man inside. The people in that club would talk about the music for the rest of their lives—the music of that one magical night.

Then, he felt a ripple. One of the dark children had pulled back. There was still no threat, but the music didn't hold them all, and so, Blind Johnny shifted his concentration. It lessened the magic of the music, but only by a degree he himself could sense. Maybe the old man inside, sending the notes back at him, felt it too. Maybe he'd make up the difference.

Amethyst didn't follow the old man, or creature, into the alley. She noted where he'd entered, and she held back. She considered, briefly, just entering through the front of the club, finding Vein, and telling him why she was there. If it had just been Vein, or Bones, or Bruno, she'd have done it without a second thought. It was Kali that held her back. The quest was important, and it was important that the girl feel as if, at the very least, the majority of what was to come was her alone.

So Amethyst waited. She pulled back into the shadows of the alley, not far from where the thin, blind man had stood so recently. As she watched, and waited, she pulled a small amulet from her pocket. One side was polished to a mirror finish. She held the chain in her hand and breathed on the surface. She took one nail and etched a symbol on the surface, then waited. Five dots appeared on the surface. One was black as pitch and looked as if someone had taken an arc welder to the metal, chipping a bit from its surface. The other four glowed very lightly. All were red. She wished there were six.

Cleo stood at her feet, tail wrapped around Amethyst's legs. The hair on the big cat's neck and tail was puffed, and her eyes glittered. Amethyst leaned down and stroked her back, keeping her eyes on the surface of the amulet.

"Where are you, Donovan?" she whispered.

Almost as if someone had heard her, one of the four red spots faded to a yellow glimmer, and moved slowly off to the side of the others.

"Here we go," she said. She heard the music from the club, and something else—something raw and clear. The black chip on her amulet began to pulse.

Vein rose from the table slowly. He didn't want to distract the others, and he didn't want to detract from the show. He only felt that it was time to make contact with someone live and warm and willing. They had come out for a night on the town, but they had also come to hunt, and to feed. If they got drawn into the performance, they could lose the night quickly, and if they started too late, hunting grew risky.

He was already breaking most of the rules he'd learned to survive by.

He was in a strange place, on unfamiliar ground, getting ready to feed. As much as he rebelled against them, he knew the rules had been conceived over centuries, and that they were born of a wisdom he hadn't yet attained. That was the rub—he needed to survive long enough to work it all out on his own.

The bar had a line of wooden stools running along its length. Most of them were full, but at the end of the counter nearest the back wall of the club, a small group of young women had pushed one stool aside and stood in a group, glancing over their shoulders at the stage. They wore too much makeup, and Vein smiled as he noticed they all wore black.

He slid past the girl nearest the center of the bar, leaned over, and waved at the bartender. The man finished polishing the glass in his hand, and stepped over. He only half paid attention, as his concentration was focused on the stage.

"Another glass of wine," Vein said quietly. "And whatever these ladies are having…the next one is on me."

The bartender turned then, and gazed at him in frank appraisal. Vein smiled and winked. The man glanced at the three girls, who'd turned to check out the offer.

"We're drinking wine," the closest girl said. She grinned flirtatiously. "I was having Chardonnay, but that red looks good."

The bartender shrugged. He brought another bottle of the house red—a rich merlot—and three more glasses. Vein took the bottle, paid the man, and turned to pour.

"I've never seen you around here," the first girl said. "I'm Monica. This is Jen, and Kathy." She waved at her friends, but kept herself pressed as close to Vein as possible.

"You probably won't see me here again," Vein said. "We're passing through." He nodded toward the table, where Bones had shaken himself free of the music's spell and turned his way.

"So, a one-night-only special?" Jen asked.

"You might say that," Vein said. "Drink up ladies. If you don't mind, I'm going to bring my friends over … there's not room for any more at that table, and I think it's easier to talk here. Don't want to disturb the show."

That's how they worked. They'd played the same scene a thousand times in San Valencez over the years. It was risky, because these girls didn't know who, or what they were going in, but it never took long to get to the point. Bones stepped up beside the third girl, Kathy, brushed against her arm, leaned in, and whispered something. She laughed.

Bruno loomed over them, and if they'd had their looks alone, things might have deteriorated, but they were so much more. The closer they circled around their new companions, the easier it was to influence them. Kali got into the act, complimenting them on their clothing, makeup, perfume, even leaning in so close to whisper to Jen that Vein was sure she'd licked the girl's ear.

And at last, he broke the brittle glass cover over their reality. He told the girls what they needed. He promised them the party of their lives. He promised them wine and sex and they hung on every word. Their hearts beat faster, their veins ran hot with fresh, wine-flavored blood, and all the while the music rolled and swelled around them like a dark lake of sound.

Vein didn't let it go on too long. He steered the talk, and the group, toward the door at the back of the club. The girls clung to them, one on each of the men, with Kali slipping in and around, keeping them smiling and laughing and confused. As the man on the stage broke into an eerie rendition of Robert Johnson's "Hell Hounds on my Trail," they pressed open the back door of the club, glanced back once, and stepped out into the night. As they turned toward the end of the alley, and the streets beyond, Vein saw a dark figure peel from the darker shadows to stand in their path. He held a guitar in his hands, and something about the way he moved shot through Vein like shards of ice. Then, the man began to play.

Donovan climbed the steps from an old, boarded-over basement shop up to an alley just off Beale and glanced up and down the street. There were cars rolling slowly by, lights flashing and all around him people moved, laughed, talked and bustled from club to club. He heard music from several directions at once, and just for a moment he stood, taking it in. Asmodeus did not take immediately to the sky. The old bird sat cautiously on Donovan's shoulder, his head cocked as if it heard something too.

Then Donovan sensed it. He couldn't sort it out, but he felt energy massing—dark energy, and other, more familiar ripples. He turned his head and glanced up at the bird, which still looked nervous.

"I think we'd better hurry, my friend. Something crazy is about to happen, and if we aren't quick, we're likely to miss it."

He didn't need anything to help him find his way. He sensed Amethyst and Cleo, and they were close. He walked the street, glancing down each street and alley, until he came to the one that led straight through to "Something Blue."

He stopped at the end of the alley and listened. Despite the cacophony of sound surrounding him, he heard the strains of the blues leaking from the alley and sliding over the walls. It stood the hair on his arms on end.

"I haven't heard anything like that in a very, very long time," he said to no one in particular. Then he stepped into the alley and hurried through toward the club. As he went, Donovan brushed his fingers over the brick wall to his left. He sensed that others had passed that way recently. He felt Amethyst, Cleo, and one other—one very dark other. He shivered.

He reached the end of the alley and glanced to either side. There was no one in sight. Music poured in a steady stream from the doorway ahead.

"Where are you?" he whispered. Even as he asked the question he wasn't certain if he meant Amethyst, Vein and his followers, or the dark other that he felt so clearly. They were all too close together for him to make distinctions, and that made him nervous. The club was packed. Anything too crazy was going to endanger innocent bystanders and draw unwanted attention.

"Guess I'm going in," he said to Asmodeus. "Watch the alley."

The bird didn't hesitate. It launched, circled once, then shot into the sky. Donovan squared his shoulders and entered "Something Blue."

CHAPTER EIGHTEEN

Vein felt the change in the alley instantly. He thrust the girl he'd held close, Jen, back toward the club. He managed to whisper hoarsely.

"Run."

She did. The others had released their companions as well, and the three girls backed toward the rear door of "Something Blue" in shock. They'd had enough wine to be tipsy, and not enough to dull their reaction to the intruder, and the strange shift shimmering down the alley's length.

"What the hell is this?" Bones asked, stepping up beside Vein. Bruno flanked him on the other side, and Kali hung back, a bit more cautious.

"Damned if I know," Vein said, but look around you. "Whatever that thing is down there, it's not your dime-store variety blues man. Are those strings silver?"

Blind Johnny stood, left knee bent, right leg straight, the old guitar tilted up at a forty-five degree angle toward the moon. Each time he stroked the strings, the alley before him changed. Years melted away. Some of the walls dissolved into shadowy, mist-images, while the alley itself widened into a street. It was paved in cobblestones, and the glow of the nearly full moon competed with the soft, hissing illumination of gas street lights.

Blind Johnny took a step forward, entered the area affected by his music, and he changed as well. His bony frame filled out, though not too far. His rags became creased black pants, his shirt white, button-down linen. He tipped his hat back, and the pits that had held white, sightless globes were gone. He was still blind, but now his eyes were dark brown coated in a white milky film. Johnny was black, but not like the man in the club. His skin had a light, copper color and his grin was wide. Under any other circumstances it would have set them at ease. In that eerie, dead-world darkness, it was chilling.

"Who are you?" Vein asked, taking a step forward from the others. "What do you want?"

"You come to my street," Johnny said, his words clipped, but almost sing-song. "You come to my street—my favorite joint—and you waltz out de back door with girls under my watch, and then you asks me, what do I want? What did you want, bloodsucker? What did you think—no one would know? That no one sees you slinking around the shadows?"

"I don't see anyone slinking, except you," Bones said. "You're back here playing to the rats in the alley, and we're slinking? We walked out the door."

Blind Johnny smiled.

"Didn't come to talk no how," he said. "You climbed down the wrong rat-hole, and I'm your Pied Piper, son."

He flicked his fingers over the strings. Vein caught a movement out of the corner of one eye. Something small and very close to the ground. Then another and another. They squirmed and climbed and dangled from the lids of wooden barrels and piles of refuse that had not been there a moment before. It was a dark tide of teeth and fur, and it was closing in fast.

"Rats," he said, loud enough for the others to hear. "Both sides."

"I see them," Kali said. She put her back to the others and turned, side to side, watching the oncoming tide of vermin.

"They like you," Johnny crooned. He strummed a cord, and the sound rippled through the flood of rats, parting them and rearranging them, drawing them out and onward. "I don't. Seen your kind before, too many times. Leave dead husks behind, steal lives and souls, and think you're going to live forever. Welcome to the edge of forever, bloodsucker. I think it's time for Johnny to play. Been a while since anyone dropped by that needed a good song."

He turned his hat brim down again and started to play. It was a sultry, delta-blues backbeat, syncopated with long, slender fingernails slapping on polished wood. Vein knew that whatever was coming, it was going to be a hell of a lot worse than a flood of ghost-rats, so he did the thing that came most naturally to him. He crouched, and he sprang.

He was fast. Even Bones and Bruno, who were used to him, were left behind as he flashed down the street that had been an alley. Blind Johnny never looked up from where his fingers danced over the strings. Instead, he began to croon, low in his throat. His vocals blended with the rhythm of the chords and notes, no words spoken, but sound that blossomed full-blown between the notes and danced there, rippling with energy.

Then he glanced up. Vein was maybe a yard away, coming fast. Johnny struck the strings a flat-slap on an "E" chord and he matched that note, his voice strong, mellow, and solid as a slab of stone. Vein hit a wall of sound that rippled as he collided with it, bent, but did not break. It flung him back a few feet, and he lunged again, trying farther to the left, looking for an opening. It wasn't there. As Johnny broke into the first verse of his song, the air between them thickened. The blues man stared at him through sightless eyes and his grin widened.

"The blood's as thick as syrup,
And it smells so sweet,
The blood's as thick as syrup,
Such a tasty treat.
But that blood you seek is all mine,
That warm blood and all its heat..."

As the words joined the chords, Vein was driven back. He skittered along the wall of sound, leaped and tried to clear it, only to be driven back and down. Every line of lyrics pushed him closer to the others, and they had problems of their own, circled against the horde of slinking, oil-black rats.

Vein turned and let the music carry him. If he couldn't attack the source of the magic, then they needed to escape, and that meant getting back to the others, and then out. As he neared them, he leaped again, clearing them easily, and drove at the far end of the impossibly aged street. Behind him, Johnny's blind eyes tracked him, and the grin widened yet again. The old man pulled up on the neck of his guitar, and the road in front of Vein curled up and back. He slammed into it, unable to stop his forward momentum quickly enough, and crashed back with a cry of pain and rage.

They were trapped. He backed into the circle with the others, watching the encroaching ring of rats warily.

Then something changed. Where the road stood up like a wall before him, a wavering, brilliant point of light appeared, dead center. The dirt of that road started to fall away, crumbling back to the dust from which it had risen. Seconds later, stepping through the portal the falling earth created, Amethyst entered the alley. Something small and dark darted past her feet, and then, with a shudder, the road closed again, and she was trapped inside with them.

"What are you doing here?" Vein growled.

"I could ask you the same question, but it's not the time," Amethyst said. "We have to take old bad and blue over there down fast, or none of us is getting out of here."

There was a howl of rage, and they both turned. Cleo, glowing with a strange, orange light that emanated from her eyes, had advanced on one side of the ring of rats. Her hair stood on end, and her tail was puffed like the spines on a hedgehog. Somehow, she had grown. She stayed low to the ground and advanced on the rats. They held their ground, glaring and unblinking, but as she drew closer, they stopped their advance. Then, like a bolt of fire, she pounced. Rats flew in every direction, some running, others tossed and batted by her claws. She cut a wide swath through their ranks to the right side of the group, and the others scattered.

Amethyst and Vein turned, to face Blind Johnny. He wasn't smiling, but he wasn't backing away, either.

"New girl in town," he said. "Looks like Johnny has a full house. Afraid you only made it for the curtain call. See, I got to *bury* these bloodsuckers. No way they walk back out into my town."

Amethyst cursed under her breath. She hadn't packed or planned for this. She whipped out the shield crystals and started spinning them, but she knew it wasn't enough to protect the others, and she didn't know from which direction to expect the attack. Behind them, rolling up again, and higher, curling in, the dirt road began to block the moonlight.

Kali cried out.

"The road! It's going to fall on us! He's going to bury us all."

Johnny raised his hand and held it above his head, the guitar held at the ready.

"One more song," he said, "before I sleep."

"Johnny!"

The voice came from behind the guitarist, and he hesitated. He half turned, but did not lower his hand.

Donovan stepped into sight at the end of the alley. The music faltered, just for a second. Vein and Bones, sensing the shift in the energy holding them at bay, drove forward. The music still held them, but they made progress, one on each side, and suddenly Bruno, with a primal scream of rage, charged up the center of the alley between them, and Kali, finding her anger at last, followed. When Bruno struck the wall of sound, Kali ran up behind him, leaped, kicked off his shoulder and dove into the music.

She slowed…stopped, actually hanging in the air…and seemed to swim through some invisible ether, clawing her way forward.

Johnny whipped back and struck a chord. He started to launch into another verse—a chorus that would crush them and free him to face the new challenge Donovan presented, but something dark and fast as lightning dropped from the sky above. He reacted, but not quickly enough. Asmodeus shot in, gripped a silver "e" string in his talon, and launched, kicking off the body of the guitar. The string stretched. For a moment it seemed it might snap, then Asmodeus released it and shot away again.

The string whipped back, slammed into the body of the guitar and twanged a loud, dissonant wave of sound. The road rippled. The alley came into sight, and then slipped away again. Johnny pressed his hands to the strings, growled, and turned fully to face Donovan, ignoring the others.

His fingers were thin and blindingly fast. When the image of the road slipped, so did the façade of his suit and hair. His eyes returned to the blind white orbs they'd been; his clothes grew ragged. His song, conversely, picked up speed and strength. His old fingers flew. A hazy wall formed at his back, and though Donovan had seen the others closing in, he and Blind Johnny stood alone, facing one another.

Donovan was tall. His hair blew about his shoulders, and his long, dark jacket hung open. If someone had seen him, just in that instant, he might have resembled a gunslinger. His hand was poised near his hip, and he turned, giving the old dead musician the smallest physical target possible.

"Show's over, Johnny," he said. "It's time to go back to sleep."

"Step aside, witch," Johnny hissed. "This ain't your fight. These are Johnny's streets; got to take care of business, and got no beef with you."

"I'm afraid that's not true," Donovan said. He'd been working something slowly out of his pocket, and he held it up. He glanced right, and left. Where he stood, the alley ended. It was bisected by another, older and smaller path, barely a walkway down the side of the club to the street. "Those beyond you are my friends. They are not yours to take. This is not your night."

"You can't stop it," Johnny said, fingers still dancing on the strings. "You and your pet crow are too late to the show. The song is nearly sung."

Donovan didn't answer. He twisted his wrist, and the item in his hand, the small pouch that Bullfinch had given him, flicked open. Dust spun into the air and dropped at his feet, and Donovan began to speak. He spoke low and fast, and the dust spread—right, left, ahead and behind. It glittered like dark diamonds, and then, as the chant continued, it began to glow.

Donovan glanced up and caught Johnny's gaze a final time. The dead man's fingers never faltered, but some of the cockiness had left his stance. The glittering, glowing trail of dust slid toward him, gaining speed.

"Ashes to ashes," Donovan said softly. "Dust to dust. I stand at the crossroads, Blind Johnny Jones. I stand at the crossroads, and I'm calling you home."

Johnny wavered. He stumbled forward a step, caught his balance, and clung to the guitar.

"No." Johnny said.

The notes had stopped, and he exerted all his strength to hold his ground. The dust at his feet wound up his ankles to his legs and drew him forward. On the ground at Donovan's feet, directly in the center of the small crossroads created by the alleys, it whirled and lifted from the ground. First it bent right, and left, dancing like a tiny tornado. It leaned, just for an instant, toward Donovan himself, and then, as if drawn to a powerful magnet, it curled down the alley toward Blind Johnny.

"Hounds on your trail, Johnny," Donovan whispered. "Give 'em hell for me."

What happened next was sudden, violent and absolute. Shooting from the alley behind, Vein broke through the last of Johnny's wall of sound. He saw the old blues-man and acted. He dove and crashed into the eerie, too-thin form and drove him forward. Johnny fell with a wail that was half song and half the cry of a damned soul. He turned in the air, and the dust whirled around him. It spun him into a glittering cocoon in just a few seconds, and then, with a blast of silence that deafened them all, it sucked him down and in. All that remained on the floor of the alley was a blackened mark where it seemed the ground had been scorched.

Donovan glanced up. Vein had fallen, but rose quickly, and the others closed in around him. Amethyst hung back, leaving Donovan to handle the moment.

"What are you doing here?" Vein asked, breaking the silence. "This is a little bit too much for a coincidence. Did Johndrow send you? Doesn't he trust me?"

"Not Johndrow," Donovan said. "Vanessa spoke to me, and it's not about trust. She cares about you. I would not have shown myself at all, if no need had arisen, but as it turns out, it's good that I came."

"We'd have beaten him," Bones said.

"I don't know about that," Donovan said. "Johnny has been dead a long time, and it hasn't slowed him down much. He's not what I mean, though. We have to talk. It seems that there's a great deal more to your quest, Kali, than any of us understood. I have some bad news, some good news, and a few thoughts to share, and I don't think the back alley of a Memphis juke joint is the place for it. Coffee?"

Vein started to puff up and bluster, then, seemed to think about it. He slumped, just slightly. He stepped forward, and extended his hand.

"Beer, or wine, if you don't mind," he said, "and since, again, I seem to have been able to put the fact you saved my ass out of my mind too quickly—thanks. That was some weird *mojo* back there. Maybe someday, when this is all over, you can tell me just what that guy—thing—was, and what you did to stop him."

"I'd like that," Donovan said. Amethyst stepped forward then, and hugged him.

"You sure took your time," she said.

"Nothing like a dramatic entrance."

Just then, as if on cue, Asmodeus dropped to his shoulder with a heavy thump, startling them all and eliciting a hiss from Cleo, who had wound her way between Donovan and Amethyst's feet. They all nearly went down in a heap.

Laughing, Donovan leaned and picked the big cat up, then turned toward the street. The others followed him as he made his way to Beale, a much more sober bunch than when they'd first hit the street, but somehow, for the first time since the quest had begun, it felt right.

CHAPTER NINETEEN

In the end, they found a couple of cups of hot coffee at a café, and several bottles of wine at a brightly lit liquor store. There was nowhere they were going to be able to get the kind of privacy they needed other than the safe house, and since the night's hunt had been interrupted, Vein and the others needed to feed.

There was plenty of room to bed down the newcomers, and the safe house was equipped for many types of visitors, including a room that easily housed Donovan, Amethyst, and Cleo. Asmodeus soared in through the doorway, circled the interior of the place slowly and settled on the top of a door frame, rustling his feathers in irritation.

"He's used to a mantel," Donovan said with a shrug. "He's very old, and set in his ways."

"I can relate," Vein said. "Let's get settled, and then suppose you tell us how you ended up in Memphis, what that thing in the alley was, and what you were talking about when you said things had changed?"

"Sounds good," Donovan said. He sipped his coffee and waited as Amethyst found a goblet, poured some wine, and curled up beside him.

The others found drinks that suited them, the vamps dosing theirs heavily from the blood supply in the safe house refrigerator. Not as tasty, perhaps, as their original plan, but more than adequate for survival. Eventually, everyone but Kali was seated. She chose to stand, pacing up and down the length of one wall and staring out toward the south.

"There is, as usual, more than one answer to a difficult question," Donovan said. "And that was more than one, in any case. As I told you in the alley, Vanessa asked Amethyst and me to trail along, just in case, but that was the entire plan. Neither of us intended to step in at all unless things got difficult."

"And she came to you because of the blood bond," Vein added. "It makes sense. I guess it's true what they say about choosing your relatives."

Donovan laughed softly. "It is a strange world, that much is certain. So, when we heard the name of the town where Kali was transformed, I knew I'd heard it before. It bothered me enough that I sent Amethyst and Cleo on ahead, and set out on my own to see an old friend. I may have more books and documents than any man on the planet, but his expertise lies in remembering what he's read. In fact, his family has kept track of supernatural history for a very long time.

"He was able to help quite a bit. As Kali can probably tell you, Old Mill, NC has had its share of strange occurrences over the years. Most of them had little or nothing to do with George Starkey, though. It's a nexus, a crossroad for lines of power. They circle the earth in every direction, large and small, and when two greater lines of power meet, that point attracts creatures of power, and extraordinary events. Old Mill is such a place. San Valencez is another. I suspect that the alley we just visited at least brushes up against the edge of a ley line."

"They attract vamps?" Bones asked. "I mean, seems like anywhere there's blood would be fine…"

"There is some kind of draw," Donovan said. "Most cities have their undead, but not all of them have the social organization of San Valencez. Your High Council is more of an oddity than you might think. I know of four others off hand. I'm sure there are more, but even those are only loosely affiliated. It might be as simple as a need to band together with other supernatural creatures. The point is, when magical things happen near crossed ley lines, the power is magnified. This makes it both more attractive to a practicing mage and more dangerous."

"Still not getting the connection to Starkey," Vein said. "He's a vamp, and from all signs, a pretty reclusive and crazy one. He doesn't seem to be much given to social interaction."

"If he was just a vampire, that would be true," Donovan said. "That's the bad news I have. George Starkey is every bit as old as you all feared. In most cases, at his age, he should be settling in and pulling back from the world. Instead, he came out of seclusion, attacked and turned Kali, and then systematically attacked those she knew and loved. It's so uncharacteristic a behavior pattern that I am convinced it's a ruse.

"You see," he said, "Among other things, George Starkey is one of the oldest living alchemists in the world."

"Alchemist?" Kali said, turning quickly. "I didn't see anything like that. All I saw was a crazy, blood-soaked killer. He killed my family. He took away everything that ever mattered to me."

"And he let you go," Donovan said.

Kali stopped—very still.

"He did not let me go," she said. "I hurt him, and I escaped."

"I don't doubt that you believe that," Donovan said. "He may even have allowed the pain, if it served his greater need. He let you get away because, as I stated earlier, his instinct is to draw back from the world. His need to feed has waned over the years. He still needs blood, but not as often, and he prefers it second-hand-distilled through one of his own.

"When George Starkey returned from London, he already had his hideout in the Great Dismal Swamp outfitted and waiting. He had a group of assistants that he turned early on, but they lacked his power, and his strength, and over time they managed to escape, or he destroyed them. Now, he is alone, and his work is incomplete. He has only earned back a few hours of sunlight a day. He is old, and he is patient. He's more than willing to work another hundred years—or a thousand—to achieve his goal, but he needs support."

"If that is true," Vein said, "why would he let Kali go?"

"He killed her family." Donovan said. "He did everything in his power to earn her hatred. He sent her out knowing that, eventually, she would try the blood quest. He is counting on her bringing help. He is hoping to control whoever returns and turn them into a new group of vassals he can send into the world for supplies—and blood. He is luring you all into a trap. At least, that is what I believe he is doing. It's also possible that the fresh blood, and the interaction with mortals, has created an imbalance in an already shaky mind. He may be as crazy as a fruit bat, but he's also dangerous, powerful, and very focused."

Kali moved so fast only Vein was able to react. She shot at Donovan, nails extending to claws and teeth bared. Her eyes were wild, and there was no sanity in her wide, glaring eyes. If Vein had hesitated, it might have been the last second of Donovan's long, interesting life.

There was a solid crack of bone on bone as Kali slammed full force into Vein, who reached up to catch her wrists and grip them tightly. She hit him so hard they tumbled back over Donovan, who managed to flip back over the couch and come up in a crouch.

"Stop!" Vein cried. His voice was powerful, almost overwhelming. He threw Kali back and dove after her, pinning her to the wall behind her before she could move back to the attack. "Have you lost your mind?"

"It's a lie," she hissed. She twisted away and tried to slip around Vein. He held her, but barely. Kali threw back her head and screamed.

"It's a lie!" she said. "He did *not* kill my family, steal my life, and set me loose like a pet dog to fetch for him. It's a lie!"

"Let her go," Donovan said. His voice was calm. He stood straight now, and he held a small amulet in his hand. "She has the right to be angry."

Vein stepped back, but not too far. Kali took a step toward Donovan, who held his ground. Amethyst was up as well, and Cleo stood on the arm of the couch, her hair on end and her eyes like glowing coals.

"Calm down all of you," Donovan said, his voice even. He met Kali's gaze steadily. "It's natural to be angry, but remember, that's what he wants. He wants you so angry that you won't think about it. He wants you too angry to do anything but come back and try and destroy him."

Kali stopped, but her fists were clenched, and her expression hadn't changed.

"I am not someone's toy," she said.

"I never said you were," Donovan replied. "I said he wants you to be. I know this is your fight. He bound you to his blood, and he abused that bond. He stole more from you than a thousand years of blood and life could ever replace. I will do anything in my power to see that you get that moment—that revenge. Your blood, my blood. Surely you feel it?"

Something flickered across Kali's features then, and Vein's eyes widened. The oath was an old one, and, none of them, possibly including Donovan himself, had ever expected to hear it spoken by a mortal to one of the undead. Yet there it was.

"And mine," Amethyst said, stepping up beside Donovan.

Vein slid his arm gently around Kali's shoulder.

"And mine…" he said.

They all stood very still. Bones and Bruno hung back. They shared a bond with Vein, but not strong enough, yet, to have bound them to Kali. They knew that something strange and powerful was happening, and that, in their own way, they were part of it. They also knew not to interfere.

Suddenly, Asmodeus launched from his perch above the door. He swooped low, circled Donovan and Amber once, and then glided across the room. With a heavy thump, he landed on Kali's shoulder. He turned and glared at her, as if adding his oath. Kali tensed, and Donovan readied himself to intervene, but then, as suddenly as it had begun, the tension broke. Kali took a step back. She brought her hand to her mouth and shook her head. Vein turned and stared at her. He moved as if to remove the old crow from her shoulder, but she backed away and shook her head harder.

Her expression had shifted to one of deep pain. She stared first at Vein, and then Amethyst, then swiveled that tortured gaze back to Donovan.

"What should I do?" she asked. "What can I do? What can…we…do?"

"That is something we will have to decide as a group," Donovan said, relaxing a little. "The fact that we will not go in unprepared is in our favor. The fact that he, probably, doesn't know I am coming, or that Amethyst is with me, is definitely in our favor. If we can even out the magical energy, the quest becomes what it was meant to be. He's old, and he's powerful, and he has two advantages you can count on him leaning on."

"Two?" Vein said.

"Yes. He has the advantage that most truly evil beings count on most. He doesn't care about anything but himself and his goals. No one is sacred to him. If his mother stood in his way he would walk over her back without even glancing down. Nothing is beyond him, nothing is too vile or too far over the edge, and he would sacrifice anything but his own existence to reach his goal. That is the first.

"The second is also part of our strength. He created Kali, so the blood bond between the two of them is strong. He is very powerful, and we now share that blood bond. At least, four of us do. That means we have our own secret weapons, as well."

He glanced over at Bones and Bruno.

"Assuming they are willing to sacrifice themselves for the cause."

"In for a penny," Bones said, grinning, "in for a buck."

"That's pound," Vein said.

"I hate that limey crap," Bones said, laughing.

Bruno didn't say anything, but he met Donovan's gaze steadily, and there was no give.

"I think, then," Donovan said, "That we have a lot of talking and thinking to do. We're about to attempt something that centuries and the Black Plague failed to accomplish. We'd better be certain we're ready."

They returned to their seats, and their drinks. They discussed what Donovan had learned, and what Kali knew, and they finished the coffee and the wine. Then, they split up and retired to their private chambers and thoughts. Amethyst curled up beside Donovan and wrapped her arms around him.

"So what do you think?" she asked.

"I think we have our work cut out for us this time. I'm old…he's much older. He wrote some of the most important documents that I've collected, and he did that *before* he died."

"I keep thinking about the story of his surviving the plague," Amethyst said, her voice growing distant and sleepy. "Too bad we can't bring back the rats for a second round."

"Yes," Donovan said, drifting off toward darkness. "That would be poetic. But if it's all the same to you, I think I've seen more than my share of rats for one trip."

As he slipped into dreams, he saw a coffin, sliding across the ground. He approached it, and realized it was not sliding, but being carried. It rode on the backs of a sea of rats.

CHAPTER TWENTY

They all slept through the morning. Amethyst was up first, and she went for coffee while Donovan went over everything a final time and tried to work out a plan. They'd already agreed that it was best if they all remained separated as they approached Old Mill. The others would rise in the evening and get back on the road. They'd covered all that needed covering before dropping off to sleep.

Amethyst had shown them the amulet she'd used to track them. She'd given a similar amulet to Vein.

"This will only work for you, or for Kali," she'd said. "It is powered by the blood bond. It will detect Starkey, too, but if you aren't careful, he'll be able to tap into it and use it against you."

"He's going to know we're coming," Bones said. "All of you are bound to him."

"There are ways to prevent detection," Donovan said. "We'll make use of them when the time comes. The bond is our advantage, and our disadvantage, and we have to use it wisely. When Amethyst and I arrive, we will be blocked. You won't sense us, but we'll let you know where we are. We have Cleo and Asmodeus, and there are other ways.

"I will have to be most careful of all, because he will detect any untoward use of magic. He's been in that same place for so long, he'll be particularly attuned to it. I'm going to go in ahead and try to find a base of operations. There's a man there who might be able to help, and a woman, Nettie, who is powerful in her own right. I'm told they can be trusted. When I have a place, I'll call Amethyst. You can meet her in a town named Rocky Mount, where the train will arrive. He's only expecting Kali and her escort, however large that might prove to be. He's expecting young, hot-headed vampires. That's what he should detect, if anything. We will remain shielded as long as possible. By the time you reach me, I'll have wards in place. If we're lucky, it will put him a little on edge. He's not used to losing track of anything, and he's not going to expect any surprises. He thinks he's setting a trap."

"Isn't he?" Kali asked.

"It's easy to catch someone who doesn't know the danger they're in," Amethyst had said.

"That's assuming he's not smarter than we are," Bones said. "From all you've told us, I'd say we'd be pretty stupid to assume he isn't."

Donovan glanced at the young vamp with a slightly improved level of respect.

"That might be the wisest thing any of us has said."

That was how they'd left it the night before. Donovan could only hope that things went—at least in the beginning, according to their plans. Now it was time for action. The others would rise in the early evening and hit the road. Amethyst had rescheduled the train, and was packed, including a new crate for Cleo to get her on board. They would all arrive in less than two days. Before they did, Donovan had a lot to accomplish, and he knew he wasn't going to be able to do it alone.

He pulled out a slip of paper from one of the pockets of his jacket. There were two names, and a phone number inscribed in Bullfinch's even, careful script. Cletus J. Diggs was the first name, and it was beside the phone number. The other name was simply "Nettie." Donovan had heard of Nettie before, though what he knew was vague. The man, Diggs, he didn't know, but Bullfinch assured him the connection was his key to Nettie's whereabouts.

"Let's just say, they're close," Bullfinch had said. "If you mention my name, he'll help you. One of his many talents is digging up strange stories for the tabloids. You'd recognize his stories as those that seem a bit too close to the truth. I've helped him a time or two with research he couldn't manage through the Internet or the resources available in Old Mill. He'll help you. He'll want to know what's going on, and if there's a story to be had, you might want to share it with him when it's all over. He's a good man, and a good resource."

Donovan had taken the card, and now he pulled out his phone and dialed.

A deep, gravelly southern voice answered on the third ring.

"Cletus J. Diggs, common law lawyer, man of the cloth, private investigator and paranormal investigator."

Donovan pulled the phone from his ear and stared at it for a moment, grinning, before speaking.

"Mr. Diggs," he said, "A mutual friend of ours, Geoffrey Bullfinch, suggested I get in touch with you. Is this a good time?"

"You got money, it's always a good time. If you're a friend of Jeff's, call me Cletus. What can I do for you Mr…?"

"DeChance. Donovan DeChance. I'm afraid what I need may sound a little strange to you. I need to find a place, and I need to find a person. The place I'm hoping you can help me find."

"And the person?" Cletus said.

"Is Nettie," Donovan finished.

This was followed by a sharp intake of breath, and a long silence.

"Haven't seen Nettie in quite some time," Cletus said at last. "Not sure I want to see her. What kind of business are you bringing my way, Mr. DeChance? Every time I cross that old woman's path, something bad happens."

"Something bad is happening already," Donovan said. "I understand you're no stranger to that sort of thing. There might be a story in it."

"Might?"

"Let's say the story depends on how things play out. The other party involved might not be very forthcoming with details…"

"Christ," Cletus said. "Guess I'd better circle the wagons and stock up on beer. What is it about this place, Mr. DeChance? It's a quiet little town on the edge of a swamp. Why does it always feel like I'm standing on the edge of some kind of big, black pit?"

"There are a lot of pits," Donovan said. "The most interesting lives are lived walking around the rims. I'll be in town this afternoon. Where can I find you?"

"There's a club in town called The Cotton Gin. I'll be in a booth in back."

"How will I know you?"

"Something tells me I'll know you."

Donovan laughed and hung up.

CHAPTER TWENTY-ONE

The Cotton Gin was tucked back off of Highway 17, just outside Old Mill on the way north toward Elizabeth City. By day they served burgers, fries, steaks and beer. At night the whiskey flowed, the jukebox kicked, and every redneck in fifty miles made their way to the parking lot, in the doors and bellied up to the bar. When Donovan stepped out of the woods beyond the cotton field that bordered the parking lot on the southern end, he stopped to study the place from a distance.

It was late afternoon. The day crowd had started to thin out, and it wasn't yet time for the after work beer drinkers to arrive. There were only a few vehicles in the parking lot. Donovan concentrated for a moment, thinking back to his phone call with Cletus J. Diggs, and smiled. A beat up old Ford Bronco parked in the far corner, away from the building, caught his eye.

"You'd better wait out here for me," he said, lifting Asmodeus carefully from his shoulder. "Should be able to find something to keep you busy with all the trees and land out here. Maybe you could chase a hawk?"

The familiar gazed at him, and for just a second Donovan would have sworn the old bird grinned. Then, with a squawk and a flutter of wings, Asmodeus took to the sky, and Donovan started across the field to The Cotton Gin.

The sun was high, and though it was getting on toward the end of September, the air was warm. Donovan always carried a small charm in his jacket that helped regulate the temperature around him. Sometimes all the advantage one needed was to not appear sweaty in hot sunlight, or to walk around in the winter without adequate clothing. It was a distraction, and distraction was half the key to magic.

No one was in the parking lot as he passed through. Donovan walked up to the front door, smiled at the "No Shirt, No Shoes, No Beer" sign, and pushed through into the club's shadowed interior.

A long bar ran across the center of the back wall. To the right were pool tables, pinball machines, and a sign pointing to the rest rooms. To the left, a scuffed dance floor fronted a small, darkened stage. Beyond that there were booths, and a few tables. In the booth farthest to the back, a man sat watching the door.

Cletus J. Diggs was a tall man. His hair was dark and reached the collar of a worn, chambray shirt. He wore blue-jeans and boots, and a sort of shapeless hat that might once have been an over-sized fedora. There was a folder open on the booth's small table, and a half-full glass of beer sat beside it. As Donovan approached, Cletus stood.

"Mr. DeChance?" he asked.

"Donovan. Call me Donovan. I'm not big on formality."

"Suit yourself," Cletus grinned. "Donovan it is. Might make it Donny—you'd stand out in a crowd a whole hell of a lot less, I can tell you. Not a lot of Donovan's in these parts."

Donovan slid into the booth across from Cletus and glanced down at the folder on the table.

"Been working a bit," Cletus said. "I wear a lot of hats, ordained minister, journalist, common law lawyer, investigator, but there's really only one thing I do. I collect information. I retain things better than most folks, and I see connections. Don't know if it's a talent, a gift, or a damn nuisance, but there it is. I've been cataloguing strange events and filing them for a couple of decades now. Sometimes it makes a story, and I write it. Sometimes, a fact, or an article comes back to me when I'm trying to figure something out years later. I should probably scan it all, but…"

Donovan laughed and waved to the waitress, who came over with a big smile. He ordered a pitcher of beer and another glass, and then turned back to Cletus.

"Cletus, you and I have more in common than you may know. Let me ask you…do you have boxes and crates and shelves filled with your information?"

"I have an entire double-wide trailer busting at the seams with it," Cletus admitted. "Collecting it I'm good at, and remembering it, but filing? Not my forté, as they say."

Donovan shook his head. "Remind me to tell you about my home, one day," he said. "I have a similar dilemma, though what I collect is much older, and usually in the form of a book, or a scroll. In any case, I hope you can help me with my business here in Old Mill. I'm a long way from California, and I'm afraid I don't have a lot of time."

"When people say that, they mean something bad is coming," Cletus said, sipping his beer. "I'm going to assume, since Bullfinch sent you, that you are one of the good guys, but in my experience folks like you only show up when something dark is in the offing. Don't suppose you can fill me in? Not sure I can be much help, or what you need, but I'll do my damnedest."

"I'll tell you what I can," Donovan said. "It might be you know more than you think. How long did you say you'd been keeping those records?"

"Lived here all my life," Cletus said. "My oldest notebook dates from when I was eight. Saw a couple of teenagers slip off into the woods. Then I saw another guy. Seemed odd to me, and I couldn't let it go. I went in after them all. I didn't go fast enough. When I caught up, the boy was face down, dead in the muck, and the girl was gone."

"What did you do?"

"Went to the sheriff…only thing I could do. Told them what I saw. They asked for details. They wanted to know did I know the guy, did I see his face, his hair, his shoes…I didn't know any of it. They never found that girl, and I never forgot. Since then, I can't seem to help myself. I see things, and I can't forget them. I write down everything. It's not just people, or places—books, newspapers, crap I find on the Internet…"

"You don't want them to ask anything you can't answer," Donovan said.

"You got it. I've made it my business to know things. It's not always a good thing, but it's what I got."

"So that must have been a while back. You were eight? That means…"

"I'm thirty-eight," Cletus said. "It was thirty years ago, and yes, I've been paying attention most of that time. I've been away a few times, of course, working on articles, taking some college courses. I keep busy."

"You'd remember what I'm here about," Donovan said. "You remember a girl who disappeared on her way home one night. Her brother was killed in a graveyard, and…"

"And her family was killed, all of them," Cletus said. He sat back and took a long pull on his beer, then poured another. "What do you know about the girl, Alicia? Do you know where she went? Who took her?"

"One thing at a time, Donovan said. "After the family was killed, were there any other disappearances? People who just didn't show up one day, trouble in the graveyard, killings?"

"This is North Carolina," Cletus said. "We're a skip and a holler from The Great Dismal Swamp, where people have been dumping bodies since Washington was yachting on the Potomac. There are always missing people and killings."

"You know what I mean," Donovan prodded. "Were there any more incidents that reminded you of what happened to Alicia, and her family? Things that fit the pattern? This might be very important. It might save lives."

Cletus took another sip of beer, and then shook his head. "Not really," he said. "There were shootings, stabbings, what Bob down at the sheriff's office calls 'domestic disputes,' and a whole lot of other things, but what happened to that boy in the graveyard. That was different. There was no reason. He was a good kid. The girl too—the kind you always hoped your own kids would meet and hook up with some day. The parents were good people too. No enemies. What happened to them was the most brutal thing I've ever seen, and the boy…they took his blood. Did you know that? He was white as a ghost.

"I was only a teenager, but I was part of the search party they sent out looking for the girl, and I can tell you, the whole time we were out there, all I could think of was that boy's face. He was so pale he didn't even look human."

Donovan nodded. "That's what I thought," he said. "I'm going to ask you for some help, Cletus, and I'm not going to be able to give you any real answers until what's about to happen has run its course. I can promise you that, if I'm still moving under my own power, I'll fill you in. I'll likely tell you more than you want to know, unless you stop me. Right now, I need help. Alicia is dead, but in a way, she needs your help too. There is something dark in your swamp, something very old and very powerful. If we are careful and clever, and very lucky, some friends of mine and I are going to take it out."

"Believe me," Cletus said, "when I tell you I've seen things in that swamp and this town that no living man should see and experienced things I should not have. I have felt power I can't explain, and by the grace of something, I made it through. I'm an ordained minister, according to a piece of paper tacked up on my wall, but the truth is I don't really know what I believe, other than there's a hell of a lot I don't understand, the majority of which I'm better off *without* understanding. That said, as I just explained, now that I know something is in the wind, I won't be able to let it go, so suppose you tell me how I can help."

Donovan nodded.

"Nothing too dangerous, I don't believe. I need a safe house—somewhere old, abandoned if possible, but if not I have money to buy or rent. It needs to be pretty much intact, and if possible to have a basement."

Cletus snorted. "You're kidding, right? Basement? If it drizzles here, the river rises and the drains in the streets clog. They don't call them basements here, they call them pools."

"What about on higher ground?" Donovan asked. "It doesn't have to have been a home, as long as it's reasonably habitable. If possible, it should be close to the swamp."

"Don't want much, do you," Cletus mumbled. "I might know a place. I'll have to go see a guy and make some arrangements."

"Then there's Nettie," Donovan said. "I'm going to need to find her."

"Ain't no findin' to it," Cletus said. "There's a shack out on Winding Mile Road. It's off 17, and there's not much of anything else back there. You go, you take you a bottle of whiskey, and then, you wait. If Nettie wants to talk to you, she'll come."

Donovan nodded.

"I can draw you a map," Cletus said, reaching for his folder.

"That won't be necessary," Donovan said. "I believe I can find it. Think they'll sell me a bottle at the bar?"

"Not if you ask, but maybe if I do...you go out and wait by my truck. It's..."

"The Bronco in the far corner," Donovan finished. He held Cletus' gaze for a moment, then stood and turned toward the door. He crossed the dance floor and stepped out into the parking lot without a backward glance. Less than five minutes later, Cletus followed.

Beside the old Bronco, the two stopped. Cletus handed over a paper bag with a bottle in it.

"She's particularly fond of Johnnie Walker," he said. "Good luck."

"I'll call you when I get back to town," Donovan said. "You'll know about the safe house by then?"

"Reckon I will," Cletus said.

Donovan shook his hand and smiled.

"I'll make this worth your while, Cletus. I never forget a favor."

"Favor hell," Cletus laughed. "I'm on the clock. I'll talk to you in a few hours."

Donovan nodded, and turned. As he started off across the cotton field toward the trees beyond, Cletus started to call out and tell him he was going the wrong way. Then, with a loud cry and a splash of black feathers, Asmodeus dropped from the sky and landed on Donovan's shoulder. Donovan never broke stride. He continued on toward the trees, and Cletus watched until man, and bird, were out of sight.

"I'll be double-D god damned," he said. "Here we go again."

CHAPTER TWENTY-TWO

Donovan wasted no time on finding transportation. He'd exited from a portal in the forest at the bottom of a set of ruined stairs. He thought the structure might once have been a church or a school. There was little left but a stone foundation, and the stairs, leading down to what would have appeared to have been a cellar. After what Cletus had said about basements, it seemed odd even to Donovan that they were there. Of course, they served a purpose. He walked the pattern, up and down the steps, and entered the magical doorway with Asmodeus planted firmly on his shoulder.

It was a chance he was taking. Nettie might not use the portals. She might not even know of them. Donovan had been hearing of her for a very long time, though, and he had the feeling there wasn't much within her purview that would surprise her. Once inside the corridor, he turned south, and walked at a steady pace. He let his mind grow still, and he held the bag with the whiskey against his heart. A breath of fresh air teased his hair, and he turned his head to the left. One of the many doors, lining both sides of the hallway gave off a slight greenish glow around its frame.

"There we go," Donovan said.

He stopped, turned to the door, and drew a symbol in the air between himself and the outlined frame. It shimmered, and then opened, and he stepped through again. The portal closed behind him, and he stood very still. He stood in darkness. He couldn't see, so he closed his eyes and stretched out his senses. He felt Asmodeus tense, and he willed the bird to be still.

He was in a cylinder of stone. The ground beneath him was damp. The air reeked of moss and mold. He opened his eyes, drew a small crystal from his pocket, and held it aloft. It glimmered, flickered, and then came to life with a soft glow that illuminated his surroundings. There was a flat wall on one side of the stone cylinder, and in the center of that a metal door with a wrought-iron handle rusted and flaked away in the grip of entropy. It was the entrance to a cave, or an underground shelter of some sort.

He turned and studied his surroundings more carefully. On one side he found iron rungs protruding from the stone. They were dark and slick with age, but they led up and out, and he took them without hesitation.

He breathed a short incantation in a language that was faintly bird-like in quality. Asmodeus shuffled again, cocking his head to listen. Donovan's body grew lighter. It wasn't enough to make him float, but it made the climb quicker, and it lessened the chance of his breaking loose one of the aged metal bars. A few moments later he clambered over the top rim of the strange entrance and stepped into an overgrown yard.

He stood looking at the back wall of a dilapidated shack. Weeds grew from the cracks in the lower logs, and the boards of what had once been a wrap-around porch lay in jumbled heaps on the ground. Donovan circled the building. In front, a rutted, pitted lane led off into the distance. The porch in front, unlike that in the rear, was intact. There was a small wooden table, flanked by straight-backed chairs. The dusty wooden floor was coated in about an inch of thick dust, but Donovan caught the glimmer of a circle beneath. The table, and the chairs, lay dead in the center.

"So," Donovan whispered, "I must step into the parlor."

Asmodeus ruffled his wings once, nervously, then lifted off and perched in the rafters, just outside the circle. Donovan glanced up at him.

"Keep an eye out for me," he said.

"Eye!" the crow agreed.

Donovan laughed and then, without hesitation, crossed into the circle. He brushed off the seat of one of the chairs, took a seat, and placed the bottle of Johnny Walker dead center on the table. Then, whispering a quick set of wards of his own, he leaned back, and studied the trees. He was not surprised, a moment later, when he heard a light thump.

"Good taste," the old woman said. Donovan still did not turn to meet her gaze. "I wondered when you'd get here."

"Events have kept me busy," Donovan said. "I certainly didn't mean to keep you waiting."

"Time flows as it will," she said. "Now, an hour from now, a week from now, I am here. I am always here…and never."

"So I've heard," Donovan said. In his mind, he ran over a series of simple incantations, carefully avoiding too much concentration on Nettie's words. "Shall we drink?" he asked.

Nettie laughed. Donovan turned then, and saw she'd thrown her head back in great gales of mirth. She was old, but gracefully old. Her hair was long, bone white, with dark streaks, and her hand, resting on the table, was small and wrinkled. She was ethereal, so thin she might have been bones beneath the gray, colorless robes she wore, or formed of nothing but smoke.

"I will not be trying my tricks on you," she said. "But I will drink. The land is always thirsty."

"As is the wind," Donovan answered. The words felt like ritual, and he was not certain where they'd come from, but he felt nothing dangerous in the exchange.

"You speak for the wind," she said. "Interesting. The response is automatic in those of power. It helps to know the direction one's allies, and enemies, approach from. You seek a great darkness. He is no longer of the air or water, earth or spirit. He stands between, manipulating each, but committed to none."

"You know him, then," Donovan said. "Starkey, I mean."

The old woman unstoppered the whiskey and poured it into two glasses. Donovan was certain they'd not been there when he sat down, but then, neither had the woman. The circle around them glowed softly. He took the glass she offered him and held it out over the table. With a wink that broke her face in another infectious smile, Nettie clinked her own against it.

"I think I like you, Donovan DeChance," she said. "I don't like many. There's Cletus, and the girl. Now there's you. I think we might be friends."

"I hope we will," Donovan said. "Now, though, I need information."

"Your dark children will be here soon," Nettie said. She frowned. "I can't abide them in my swamp. They steal what isn't theirs; they have no regard for older powers."

"These are different," Donovan said. "They are young, but they've seen a great deal, and we are bonded. I will speak for them."

"But…you speak for the wind," Nettie cackled. "Don't worry magic man, I'll not disturb your friends. Mind you, take them with you when you go. If you go. The one you seek would have seen a lot of sunrises, if he could. He is deranged, and doomed, but he is no fool. He will know you. He will sense you. He will feel the bond. You will have to tread carefully."

"He must have a weakness," Donovan said. "Everyone has a weakness, even those of us who have truly seen too many sunrises."

"There are never too many sunrises," Nettie said. "His weakness is his dream. He would do anything to possess it. He would sacrifice anything, everything, to achieve it. He believes that if he retains his connection to the arts, and his ties to death, and brings both into the light of day, he will transform."

"Another Philosopher's Stone," Donovan said. "He's created a new level."

"He *dreams* of a new level," Nettie said. "Never reached the last one. Philosopher's Stone was never far from his heart. In his soul, and yours. You know that, too. He gave up all hope when he stepped into the shadows."

"And yet," Donovan said, "I hear he has taken steps into the early light. I hear that he does not rest as soon as others of his kind."

"Too slow," Nettie said. "His progress is too slow. The land will survive. The sun and moon and stars, they abide. George Starkey will never find his way into the daylight.'"

"So what can I do?" Donovan said.

"Said he can't find his way," Nettie cackled. "Didn't say you couldn't lead him. He's too old, too strong. If you fight him, you might hurt him, but he will destroy you. Maybe your dark children, and that lover too," she cackled again. "You tell her she's a lucky girl for Nettie, yes?"

"I will tell her," Donovan said. "But…"

"That's enough," Nettie said. "Drink up."

Donovan didn't argue. He tossed back the whiskey. As he did, he caught a movement out of the corner of his eye. It was Asmodeus. The old crow took flight, soaring up toward the dying late afternoon sun toward the tree line across the winding drive that led back out the highway.

He'd seen the bird take flight dozens of times. It was a graceful motion, powerful and regal. Still, there was no reason it should have fascinated him. Then, shaking his head, he smiled, and turned. The bottle was gone. His glass held about two fingers of whiskey. There was no sign of Nettie, just the dusty porch, the empty chair and the whiskey.

"From wind to land," he said. He lifted the glass and downed the whiskey in a gulp.

He rose and climbed down from the porch, heading back to the old concrete opening. Asmodeus circled once, as if checking the lay of the land, then dropped to Donovan's shoulder as he swung up and over the stone lip and down into the cylindrical entrance to the portal.

"When this is all done," he said, talking to himself as much as to the crow, "we are going to have to come back here and find out where that doorway leads."

A moment later they stepped through the portal in the stone, and the late afternoon shadows were all that remained in the dark, musty chamber.

CHAPTER TWENTY-THREE

Amethyst stood outside the train station in Rocky Mount, North Carolina, Cleo tucked safely into the cat carrier and eyeing her curiously. The sun had set an hour before, and Amethyst's patience was wearing thin. She'd been waiting nearly an hour, and there was no sign of Vein and his crew.

"We should have gotten our own ride," she said, squatting down beside Cleo. "I promise, as soon as we get in the car, you're out of the box. We'll leave it right here on the sidewalk."

As if on cue, the low purr of the dark, shadowed car rolled out of the shadows. Amethyst stood and watched as Bruno pulled around the corner. The back door opened, and, as promised, Amethyst unsnapped the door of the crate and scooped Cleo up in her arms. Bruno stepped out, opening the trunk with the automatic button as he did, and grabbed her bags.

"Thanks," she said, slipping into the back beside Kali. Vein sat on the far side, and Bones rode shotgun. He turned and grinned.

"Sorry we're late. Bruno is a little overly trustful of the satnav, if you know what I mean."

"Go to hell," Bruno said, climbing back in behind the wheel.

Bones started cackling. "The damned sign said 'TRAIN'. It had an arrow man. Seriously."

Bruno ignored him and stared straight ahead, pulling away from the curb and rounding the small square back onto the street. The area was old and industrial, and the streets were narrow. There was a police department a couple of blocks down, and a Catholic school on the opposite corner.

"It's old," Amethyst said. "The city."

"This is one of the oldest parts," Kali said, speaking up unexpectedly.

"The station you just came in on is one of the Grand Central line stops. This used to be nice, at least, that's what we were taught in school. Now it's run down, overrun by gangs and drugs."

"I wonder why areas like that always seem to grow around train stations," Vein said. "It's that way in San Diego, and San Valencez, I'm betting it was the same in Memphis."

Amethyst nodded. "Pretty much. So, do we know where we're going?"

"As long as we don't need to follow any more signs…" Bones said.

Bruno lashed out then, cracking his fist into the side of Bones' skull.

"Cut it out," Vein snapped. He turned to Amethyst. "We need to get them out of this car. They're starting to go stir crazy. We have a couple of hours to Old Mill. We heard from Donovan about an hour ago, and once we get in close, Kali says she can help us find our way. He found a damn plantation house…"

Amethyst laughed. "I hope he doesn't expect me to dress for dinner."

"It's not in great shape," Kali said. "I know it. It's the old Pope Plantation. It's sort of around the side of the swamp from Old Mill, out in the middle of nowhere. There are some strange stories about that place, and way back, just after the Civil War, there was some kind of scandal with a church fire and a preacher from back north. No one goes there. Even kids looking for a good time avoided it when I lived here. There's just something—wrong—about it."

"Well, let's hope that the 'wrong' you sensed back then had nothing to do with Starkey."

Kali shook her head, almost violently. "Not him. There are a lot of strange things in that swamp; he's probably not even the oldest, or most powerful. They steer clear of one another though. He doesn't go to that place. Not sure how I feel about going there."

"If Donovan thinks that it's safe," Amethyst said, "I'm inclined to believe him. He's never steered me wrong, and he's been at this a very long time."

"How long?" Vein asked, curious.

"He may share that with you one day," Amethyst said. "It's not a story he gives up easily, believe me."

Cleo let out a soft cry at that, as if in agreement, and Amethyst laughed. "Cleo could tell you too, if she talked."

"This is the strangest road trip ever," Bones said, turning to watch the fields passing on either side. They rolled under signs leading to Farmville and Greenville. They passed horse ranches and huge, looming metal water towers.

"Something tells me," Vein said, "that we aren't in Kansas anymore."

The front of the home had only a concrete patio. The crumbled remnant of a tool shed sat to one side, and the door had the utilitarian look of a servant's entrance. In the moonlight, it was gray and lifeless.

Bruno pulled up with a small crunch of gravel, and they climbed out, spreading out through the yard and grounds slowly. Cleo leaped from Amethyst's lap and rounded the corner of the building, and Amethyst followed. They walked around the side of the house, and in back, they found Donovan leaning back in a weathered wooden rocker on a long, sweeping porch. Turning to the trees and fields beyond, Amethyst saw why the door by the drive was so utilitarian. This was the side that mattered. It faced into cotton fields that stretched off into the distance until they ran up against a line of trees on the far side. It was all a silvered chiaroscuro wash, and the shadows seemed to creep across the fields toward them.

"It must have been spectacular, back in the day," Donovan said.

Amethyst nodded, then turned. Cleo had leaped up into Donovan's lap and curled against him contentedly. A quick glance to the porch roof showed the dark shadow of Asmodeus, clutching at half-rotted wood and glaring out at the world.

"It's not exactly the Hilton," Amethyst said. "It feels…odd."

"I got a bit of the history on the way out here," Donovan said. "Mr. Cletus J. Diggs is a treasure trove of information on the area, its history, and in particular anything strange. This plantation belonged to a family named Pope. They owned the land back into Colonial times. Seems like there was a scandal when a preacher came out after the war wanting to bring his message to the freed slaves. His church was burned, him along with it, and most of his family."

"This feels like more than that," Amethyst said, running her fingertips over the porch floor. "There's something deeper."

"The scandal was only the start," Donovan said. "What came later, to this house, was the strange part. When we're done, if you're interested, we'll buy Cletus a pitcher of beer and he can tell you again, starting with the story of The Preacher's Marsh, and on through what happened to the Popes. The important thing is, none of the locals will come here, and, according to a very old lady named Nettie, neither will Starkey. Whatever it is about this place that you sense—it repels him.

"That line of trees is the edge of the swamp. If you go in about a quarter mile, it turns to marsh, but there are trails. We should be able to travel all the way from here to Old Mill if necessary without seeing any sign of civilization."

"You didn't tell me we were going hiking in a swamp," Amethyst said.

"I didn't know. I'm still hoping we won't have to. I had an interesting chat with one of the local powers that be. She was a little obtuse, but I think she may have been onto something. It's possible that we've been going about this all wrong."

"What do you mean?" Vein asked, walking over and hopping up gracefully to perch on the edge of the old porch.

"Our plans, so far, have centered pretty much on getting an advantage as we walk boldly into Starkey's lair and destroy him. Kind of like going swimming with a shark, but taking a dagger with you because you plan to kill it."

"We *will* kill him," Kali said. She appeared beside Vein so quickly it seemed as if she materialized from the shadows.

"Yes," Donovan said. "There's no way around that. I'm thinking, though, that there might be a way to get him onto more even ground. We need to draw him out of his hole and into the world where, arrogant as he is, he is less comfortable and more vulnerable."

"Easy to say," Bones said. "Dangerous creatures tend to guard their dens. My father hunted. He told me stories. The worst of those stories always started with tracking something to its home."

"My point exactly," Donovan agreed. "If we can avoid it, that's the last thing we want. He's expecting you. He isn't expecting all of us, but believe me, George Starkey is anything but stupid. He will prepare for the worst, and that means that even if we go in with all the force we can muster, and a good plan, he might just squash us like annoying swamp bugs.

"The old woman, Nettie, told me something. She said that if we wanted to draw him out, we had to give him what he wants."

"You mean Kali?" Vein asked, leaning in as if to argue.

"No," Donovan said. "I mean the secret he seeks. We need him to believe that we have what he wants more than anything else. The secret of walking by day. His new Philosopher's Stone. He believes if he can be a day walker and still retain the power of his curse, he can walk out into the world and reclaim the life he left behind so long ago. He believes he will be immortal."

"That's well and good," Amethyst said, "but unless you are holding out on our vampiric friends, we don't *know* that secret. Doesn't that put a kink in your plan?"

"Not necessarily," Donovan said. "You know what the magicians in Vegas say. It's not about what you do, it's about what you make them watch. Perception is reality. What we need is to give the illusion that we have the secret. That's all that's necessary, and, of course, we won't be *we*. He has to believe that Kali and the rest of you have the secret. We can play it against his own arrogance, if we make it seem as if Kali made off with the information she needed when she left. I think I know enough about his work, at least his early work, to give the proper impression. The key will be in pulling off the illusion."

"I hope there's a whole hell of a lot more to this plan," Bones said, turning and walking off toward the edge of the cotton field. "And what *is* it about this place?"

Donovan watched him walk away and gathered his thoughts. He thought he knew what they needed to do, but he wasn't fully prepared to explain it.

"We need to get settled in," he said. "It's not going to be horribly comfortable, but it could be worse. Cletus brought us out some cots, and blankets. This place is built on a hill, and it has something most homes around her don't. A full basement. No windows. I made sure it was sealed, and I've added some wards just to be sure. There's a room on the first floor that's intact—Amethyst, you and I will take that. Tomorrow, we're going to make our presence known."

"I thought you said he was just supposed to know *we* were here," Vein said.

"No, just that you're the ones coming for him," Donovan said. "My plan is to make it seem as if our presence is a coincidence. There are plenty of things I could be investigating, even Starkey himself, without being involved in your quest. I want his thoughts divided. Any distraction will help, and if he thinks he can get what he needs from you, he may be anxious to do so before confronting me. In any case, we need a better idea of the lay of things, and I think hitting Old Mill by day is the best way to pull it off. We'll be back early in the evening, and when we're all ready, we'll make our move."

"So soon?" Amethyst asked, surprised.

"The longer we're here," Donovan said, "the more likely he is to make the connection between our two groups. We can mask the blood bond, but only for so long. He'll sense it, and he'll feel the trap, and then we might never pry him out of his hole."

"It's going to be sunrise soon," Vein said. "Bruno, Bones, let's go get our stuff out of the car. We need to get downstairs and sealed up."

He turned to Donovan.

"I hope you know what you're doing, man," he said. "We're all counting on you now."

Donovan nodded. "I know. We'll talk tomorrow, and I'll know more."

"You got it," Vein said. He turned and slipped off into the darkness. A few moments later, he and Bruno returned, loaded down with bags. Vein and Bones followed. Kali waited for them at the top of the stairs, and then, with a final glance back at Donovan, she preceded them into the basement.

Donovan stood and carried Cleo into the old Plantation house. There was a quick flutter of darkness as Asmodeus soared in ahead of them. The place had a lingering grandeur. The Popes had left it as they'd lived in it, and no one had disturbed it. Dusty vases and crystal lamps rested on the shelves and mantel. In the dining room, there were actually plates and goblets, coated in grime, some canted to the side, set out on the table.

"I can't believe no one has raided this place," Amethyst said. "It's like visiting Pompeii."

"I don't know the entire story," Donovan said. "I did spend some time getting the master bedroom ready for us. We have well water, and Cletus brought a pile of clean bedding from a thrift store in Elizabeth City. We should be okay for a couple of nights. Not exactly camping, and you better believe we'll be setting some serious wards, but it should be comfortable. Just in case, I brought a bottle of cabernet…"

He led her around the dining room, down a short hall, and ahead, she saw the flicker of lantern light. The entire effect was eerie, like stepping into a scene from the past. The walls were papered at the top with a striped design, and from about the midpoint down, they were of polished, slatted wood. The floor was hardwood and also polished, glimmers of the flickering light caught stray patches where the dust didn't fully cover the original sheen. There was an ancient, hand-woven silk runner down the center of the hall, and pictures lined the sides.

They entered a large room with curtained windows that looked out over the fields in back of the plantation, and the swamp. The shades were drawn, and Amethyst immediately went to the largest, in the center, and raised the dark covering to reveal the moonlight-washed landscape.

Donovan came to stand by her for a moment, gazing out at the swamp across the fields.

"He's out there," she said. "He could be watching us, even now."

"I don't think he knows we're here," Donovan said. "If he does, I doubt he sees it as anything more than a minor annoyance or curiosity. What has he to fear? He hasn't been challenged in a century."

She nodded, then turned to the room. The bed was a huge, sleigh-style affair of rich mahogany. The blankets were turned back, and on a wooden desk, which still held pens and stationary from a time that was dead, Donovan had placed a bottle of wine, and two clean goblets.

Cleo had jumped up to settle into the covers, and Asmodeus, soaring low down the hall like a child's glider, had whirled up to the top of the room's great mantel. There was a fireplace, but it had been lifeless and without flame for decades.

"We have to finish this quickly," Amethyst said. "It's a beautiful old home, but…"

"I know," Donovan said. "We don't belong here. No one belongs here anymore. It will serve us, but that's another reason I want to go in tomorrow night. I'm not sure the plantation will abide our presence longer than that."

"Cheerful thought," Amethyst laughed. "How about I set the wards, and you pour some of that wine. I'm exhausted, and all I really want is to climb into that bed and try and rest."

"Rest?" Donovan asked, raising an eyebrow.

Amethyst smiled, and turned away.

"Just pour the wine, Donovan. And don't spill any on old Master Pope's papers. We wouldn't want him tracking us down in our sleep."

CHAPTER TWENTY-FOUR

Deep in the Dismal Swamp, down a winding trail that was barely discernable in the twists and turns of vines and Cypress, a concrete shelter lay buried in the loamy soil. The top was flat concrete. In the center, a hand-wheel worked the mechanism of a thick, air-tight metal door that had once been destined for the hull of a U.S .Navy ship. Vines encroached on either side, and branches had been carefully pruned and groomed to dangle over the top of it all, obscuring it from aerial view.

Beneath this, chambers branched out through the swampy water, lodged deep and watertight. It had taken hundreds of years to build, expand, seal and hide it. It was created by the hands of those long dead, enslaved, worked to death, and fed upon, their bones and blood and souls pounded into the walls and the floor.

Each new wing served a purpose.

The central chamber was round. The cylindrical entrance led down to it with a ladder of metal rungs. Four tunnels branched off, one in each of the cardinal directions. There were smaller chambers at the end of each of these. Their walls were lined with cases and stands, equipment and racks of glassware. Some were full, others empty and gleaming.

The technology was eerie. There was power. There was running water. There were analyzers, testers, gauges, a centrifuge, and even an odd computer cobbled together with thin wire, strange, bug-like components, cables and wires and a flickering monochrome monitor with pale red text scrolling across the screen.

None of it was right. It was as if everything in those walls had developed parallel to, or possibly a bit ahead of, the world beyond, but without real interaction. Books lined shelf after shelf. Benches were strewn with diagrams, schematics, formulae and records.

In the southernmost chamber, bent over a rack of beakers, a burner heating one to a boil, George Starkey watched colored liquid bubble through a glass tube. He was careful, and patient. Every few moments, he jotted notes on a legal pad that lay open before him. He never hurried. He hadn't hurried in all the years of his research. There was a single shelf at shoulder height in the main chamber. It was lined, three deep, with legal tablets like the one he wrote in. They stood on edge with their top binding out, and each held an annotation of date and subject. It was a large chamber, and there were literally thousands of pads. Each was filled with line after line of thin, spidery, eerily perfect script.

He'd created it all. He'd designed the chambers before leaving for England more than three centuries in the past. He'd taken his not inconsiderable fortune and set workers to the task of excavating, framing, and pouring the original walls of the main chamber, and he'd set sail for Europe. Since his return, he'd expanded, redesigned, and strengthened the structure. He'd extended the tunnels in each direction of the compass and built the four laboratories, using each for a different branch of study and experimentation. He had a goal. It was a simple goal, at its base, and incredibly complex in its resolution. None of this deterred him. He was focused, and he was confident. His experiments had borne fruit, and every day he felt a bit closer to completion.

He had built and designed every piece of equipment. When others had served him, he'd gained access to journals and papers, textbooks and diagrams. He'd used them to guide him, but only loosely. He knew every circuit, every wire and solder joint. He had touched every jar, container, beaker and burner. He'd recorded every waking moment. Now, after nearly a century of almost absolute solitude, he felt himself slowing.

It wasn't a noticeable change—not on a daily, weekly, or even yearly basis. Anyone observing him would have noted no discernible difference. But it was there. By his calculations, the lethargy working its way through his system would begin to take control of him in less than a century. He did not know when his research would be complete, but it seemed reasonable that it might stretch beyond that point. Withdrawing from the world was inevitable. It was the curse of the undead. As his mind and body reacted to long solitude, his metabolism slowed. He'd fought it. He'd run a side-set of experiments and found ways to prolong his energy, but the simple fact was he was fighting a principle of physics. Entropy. In the end, he would lose, unless he took action.

What he needed was fresh blood. He needed interaction, even if the minds he communicated with were inferior in every aspect, even if they had no comprehension of what he was doing. He needed the spark of life to draw him back from the brink, and the last time he'd felt that spark was before the last of his "assistants" had passed on. They had all given in, eventually. The seclusion, the quiet—they didn't have his work, or his art—and they lacked his strength. They faded. One by one they dug their own graves, or found tombs they could slip inside. They were there, and then one day, they were simply gone.

Starkey had continued, and for a very long time, barely realized they were gone. He had not gone into death and rebirth to the blood without thought or preparation. He had known the fate of the eldest of the vampire race, and he also knew that, though it would take an effort, that he could renew his vigor. The key was in his own mind, the revitalization was an effort of will. He still had what other ancients did not—a strong desire to live, and a goal.

He'd taken a rare break from his work a few years back and started frequenting the areas of the swamp nearer to civilization. He didn't venture out where he could actually be seen, but remained in the shadows. It wasn't that he feared anything from the town. Old Mill was a tiny bump in the road gathering of old homes giving way to time, and cheap, government housing that was spreading like mold. Even if someone saw a stranger hanging around the edges of the fields, or just under the branches of the first trees leading into the swamp, nothing would be said. His caution was entirely devoted to making a correct choice.

He'd watched for several weeks, and when the young girl that had first caught his eye, a girl who looked very much like the lover he'd left behind more than three centuries in the past, took off by herself through the cemetery, he'd known the time was right to strike. He'd taken her, and he'd killed her brother. At the time, he'd been angry at the intrusion, but the more he'd contemplated it, the more he saw that it fit his pattern. He'd known he would have to make the girl hate him—it was essential that she come back. What he'd not anticipated was that it would be simple, and that, once he'd begun it, there would be so much pure enjoyment in it.

Fresh blood was rich and heady. It had been so long since he'd hunted, since he'd given in to the basic craving that kept him alive and moving, that the wash of energy and heat had nearly driven him mad. When it was done, he'd barely had a clear enough head to allow the girl to escape. His mind had filled with images of young, tender skin, and, just for a moment, he'd considered putting aside his work in favor of the feast, the lust, and the carnage the shadows promised. He could have feasted well in Old Mill, for all its faults. Then he'd recovered, and the plan had unfolded as expected.

The girl, Kali, had watched him all the time. When he took her family, she tried to fight him. That was when he'd shown her a taste of the control he had on her mind, and her soul. That was when he'd forced her to drink some of the blood he'd stolen from her loved ones. He'd spoken as little as possible. He'd let her know only the hint of his plan—his dream—to walk in the light, and this he did by being out earlier, and staying out later than she could manage. He didn't push it. He gave no indication of how far along he was in his goal of watching the sunrise. Just enough to plant the germ of an idea in her mind. Just enough to give her confidence, and allow her anger to bubble up and claim her.

One day he'd gone out, and she'd sealed the shelter they'd shared tightly. She'd gone to the town, somehow stolen a vehicle, and driven it out into the swamp, ramming it against the outside door of the large, ornate tomb, and taken off with the key in her pocket, running like the night wind. He'd watched her go. When she was gone, he'd cleared away the debris and opened the tomb. He knew he'd have to come there, periodically, and leave signs of himself, so when she returned she'd believe she'd hurt him, leaving him out too long in the sunlight. She had never seen his laboratory, and it was with pleasure at a well-laid plan, and relief at finally returning to his work, that he'd turned deeper into the swamp and returned to the chambers he had so long called home to wait. He knew he'd sense her when she was near again—and others, there must be others.

The liquid bubbled through the tube, dripped into the beaker at the end, and gave off a faint, pungent odor reminiscent of wormwood. He studied it, lifted it free of the stand, and, untouched by the heat of the glass, carried it through the door and down to the next lab, where the work would continue. He didn't know when Kali would return, but he hoped she would bring an army. He had so much to do, and he needed things. He needed extended arms and eyes. He needed to find his way back to the light.

He stopped in the entrance to the eastern lab. He cocked his head and sniffed at the air. He moved the beaker to arm's length, and sniffed again. He stood very still, and then, slowly, he smiled.

"Not long," he muttered.

Then, dismissing all other thoughts from his mind, he entered the eastern lab and continued with his work.

CHAPTER TWENTY-FIVE

Donovan and Amethyst returned to the plantation house in the late afternoon, laden with packages. Asmodeus soared up and behind them, circling down toward the porch. Cleo had chosen to remain in the house, curled up on the old bed, to wait, and to watch over their charges below.

It had been a fruitful day in Old Mill. The library, a squat, brick structure, had been sorely lacking in shelf space and modern fiction, but had included a copy machine, and a small section the size of a large walk-in closet dedicated to local history and authors stretching back into Colonial times. Donovan had poured through old newspapers, reports of missing persons, maps, and property records. It had taken most of the day, but he thought he'd pinpointed the area where Starkey was most likely to have created a lab, and had found records of odd supplies being shipped in and picked up, coinciding with periods where there were steady disappearances—mostly hunters, or transients, kids roaming too far into the swamps untended.

Nothing had ever been found in the searches that were mounted. Donovan had made a copy of a topographical map of the area. With a little help from a charmed and charming lady behind the counter, he'd managed to pinpoint the locations of most of the disappearances.

"I'm writing a book," he'd explained. "I want to be sure I get the local history and layout correct."

The woman had been excited to help, and very knowledgeable on her favorite subject—Old Mill, NC.

Donovan didn't expect to find Starkey in any of the locations where people had disappeared. It made more sense that his followers would have been instructed to hunt *away* from their central location. That being the case, what he used the disappearances for was to triangulate an area that had never fallen under suspicion, far enough into the swamp not to be noticed on a casual hunting trip, or a nature hike. Starkey had been in there a long time. It would likely not take as much to reach him now as it had before more of the land had been cleared. To prevent this, the only solution would have been to own that land, and, as expected, Donovan found a large plot owned by a G. Stanley, owned for so long that the records showed generations of Stanley's renewing their lease, paying their taxes, and generally avoiding any interaction with the citizens of Old Mill that would leave an impression.

"It's very odd," the librarian said thoughtfully. "I thought I knew every family within fifty miles of here, and there aren't as many names as you'd think involved in that. I've never heard of, or met, a Stanley, but there it is. Mr. Stanley—the present Mr. Stanley—owns fifty miles of swamp land smack dab in the middle."

Donovan had chatted with the woman, while Amethyst wandered the aisles. On their way out, they'd found one last interesting tidbit tucked in the back of a cardboard box of "for sale" books near the front door. It was a poorly bound and obviously amateurish volume titled *Oddities and Strange Happenings–Being an account of twenty years of unexplained sightings, disappearances, and hauntings in or around Old Mill, NC*. It was written by a man named Normal Nixon, and the date on the publication page stated 1832. The pages were yellowed and bound with thick thread, and the entire thing was wrapped in leather-board covers.

"Are you sure you want to sell this?" Donovan had asked, turning the book over and over in his hands. "It's very old, and it seems like it ought to be shelved with the local history."

"It's all stuff and nonsense," the librarian had sniffed. "A load of manure piled in one place by my own great, great grandfather. There are better uses for our shelves."

Donovan had nodded, and handed over the $2.00 asking price without question. He noted her nametag, Iris Nixon, and wondered what old scandal had caused her to excise her own family member's book, but it was a mystery for another time.

"It looks like it might make some good light reading," he said. "Who knows, maybe I'll find something about one of the disappearances that wasn't in the official accounts."

"You'll find nothing *but* things that aren't in the official accounts," Iris had informed him. "That man was not right in the head. He claimed there were creatures living in the swamps, that we'd been visited by creatures from another planet—ghosts, vampires, you name it. You'll find all of those in that book, and more, and I'll be happy to see it gone."

Donovan had tucked the book away with the copies they'd made and their map, and thanked the librarian profusely. Donovan called Cletus, who dropped by and gave them a ride, stopping by a grocery store for wine and supplies, and then heading back out the long, overgrown road that led to the Plantation. He'd let them out a quarter mile from the place.

"Nothing personal," he said, "but I don't like getting too close to the old Pope Place. This is about where my comfort zone ends."

"We appreciate the ride," Donovan said.

Amethyst smiled. "You sure you don't want to stop in for a beer, Cletus?"

Cletus shivered and shook his head. "Not tonight, ma'am," he said. "You folks be careful out there."

With that, Mr. Cletus J. Diggs had climbed back in his Bronco and headed back toward 17 in the distance.

The short walk to the Pope Plantation had helped clear the last of the cobwebs from Donovan's mind. When they got inside, Amethyst set out to arrange the supplies they'd picked up, while Donovan spread the map on the old dining room table and opened up Normal Nixon's book.

Despite Iris' disdain, the book was carefully organized, and meticulously detailed. Each short chapter chronicled a different "sighting" or "haunting," and though the book wasn't recent enough to cover most of the disappearances he'd charted, it did mention the first few, and a number of others he was able to add to his chart, narrowing their focus yet again.

There were also several sightings of a tall, thin man with whitish-blonde hair near the edges of the swamp. Apparently Normal had a string of 'watchers' who kept an eye on things, and reported back to him. This stranger had been seen more than once, including a single entry about a delivery, by boat and "by the light of the full moon," along the in-progress Intercoastal Waterway. There were no details, but "large parcels of odd size and description were carried from the boat to land, and from there taken into the swamp on carts."

As in all the entries, Normal had come as close as possible to the coordinates of the sighting and had inscribed the time and the date. Donovan turned to the map, extending it in his mind toward where he knew the waterway to run, and made another quick annotation.

"I think that's it," he said. "This should get us close enough. Particularly if there's even a trail left where this boat landed."

"What's all this about boats?" Vein asked, slipping into the room soundlessly. One moment the two of them had been alone. The next, the vampires had joined them, and Bones, in particular, grinned widely. Apparently, he liked sneaking up on people.

Donovan filled them all in quickly.

"So," he concluded, "this area here—owned by the unseen and mysterious Mr. Stanley—has got to be where Starkey has built his laboratory. My guess is that he's sunk it into the ground. It's rough to get anything solid there, but there's a higher, raised portion near the center of this plot. Also, he's had a lot of years to bolster his foundations and reconfigure. If he has it buried, it will be easy to conceal from anyone who might happen to fly overhead, sealed against wind and weather."

"Damn," Kali said.

They all turned to her.

"What is it?" Donovan asked. "Did I miss something?"

"No," Kali said. "I did. You're saying he's had this secret place in the middle of the swamp all along? Since before I was here?"

"Probably for centuries," Amethyst said. "Remember, he came directly here from London in the 1600's."

Kali shook her head.

"The place he took me, the place we stayed while I was with him, was here," she pressed her finger into a point on one of the outer corner's of Starkey's land. "It had been a church basement, and it was surrounded by a small, ruined cemetery. It was big, and he'd cleaned it out to make a large space. There was no equipment, though. Nothing but a sealed, concreted box. When I left, I rammed a pickup truck into the front of it and left it sealed tight. He was out at the time, and I figured I'd hit him where it hurt.

"I had plenty of places to go, and to hide. I thought maybe he didn't. I thought, maybe, that if I locked him out of that place, he'd push his luck like he always did, stay out too late, and not make it back in time to find his way to safety. At the least, I figured I'd hurt him enough I might have a chance to get away. All this time, that's what I believed."

"It's in our favor now," Donovan said, keeping his voice even. He didn't want to sound patronizing, but he also didn't want to set her off again. Vein might not be fast enough to intercept her a second time.

"He knows that is what you believe. He'll expect you to return to that spot and investigate, and that's what the four of you should do, carefully. He needs to know that you are here. I suspect, at that point, he will leave you some clues to draw you farther in. I have a plan to draw him out, but it depends on him seeing you, and you getting away. We will be coming at him from the side to try and help insure that. Of course, our cover will be blown at that point, but that is fine. Here's what I have in mind ..."

Over the next half hour, Donovan outlined his plan carefully. Vein asked a few questions, and Kali chimed in to make some suggestions that improved their chance at safety. They all worried at it from every angle, but after an hour, they were in agreement.

"I think this could work," Amethyst said at last. "It's going to be touch and go near the end. We don't know how powerful he might be once he's cornered, and we don't know what safeguards he has in place. We have surprise, and we have one thing probably more important than all the rest."

"What's that?" Bones asked.

"He's arrogant," Amethyst said with a shrug. "He believes his plan is working perfectly, and he's not even considering other options or contingencies. If things had not worked out as they did, he might have been perfectly correct in his assumptions, but he's in for a surprise, and in my experience, evil arrogant geniuses don't take well to being surprised."

They all laughed at that.

"We'd better get going," Donovan said. "That water entrance is near where they built a place in the 1800s called 'The Halfway House,' between Virginia and North Carolina. Pretty rough place, back in the day."

"You know this because…" Kali said, glancing over at him.

"I was there," Donovan said. He met her gaze for a moment, and then smiled. "When this is over, if it doesn't bore you, I'll tell you about it. It's actually a pretty good story. I was younger then."

"No shit," Bones laughed.

They rose, said their goodbyes and headed out into the darkness. The young vamps took off toward the tree line and the swamp. Donovan led Amethyst around the side of the plantation house to where steps led down into a ruined cellar.

"Portal?" she asked.

"Not exactly," Donovan said. "I'm going to try something I've done once before. I'm going to *make* it a portal. It no longer goes anywhere else, so it should be possible. We are dead center on top of one of the ley lines…"

"Once?" she said softly. "So, you aren't certain…"

"Trust me," he said. When he winked, she slugged his shoulder.

"You'd just better not get us trapped in a wall of stone," she said. "I want to see how this one plays out."

A few moments later, they disappeared into the shadows. Cleo stayed behind once more, and Asmodeus, while he did not follow them into the portal, shot into the sky, headed for the swamp and was gone.

CHAPTER TWENTY-SIX

Without Donovan and Amethyst to slow them, Kali led Vein and the others through the swamp at breathtaking speed. She jumped over cypress roots, cleared small streambeds without slowing and actually leaped at one point to swing from branch to branch down a row of trees to avoid soft spots in damp soil. The others followed easily, happy to be out and stretching, clearing the cobwebs.

In a clearing about a quarter of mile from the plantation house, she stopped, held up her hand, and cocked her head. She listened, and then, very carefully and thoughtfully, took a deep whiff of the air surrounding them. She turned slowly.

"What is it?" Vein asked. He extended his own senses, feeling for any touch of the blood bond, any draw or pulse.

"Deer," she said. "Close. A small herd."

Bones laughed softly. "You want to hunt?"

Kali shook her head.

"If he was close, they wouldn't be here. We're not far from the tomb I sealed with the truck. I had to come in from the other side—no way you could drive through here—but we're near. He hasn't been staying there."

"You heard the magic man," Vein said. "Starkey has a lab. You think this tomb is still sealed?"

"I hope not," Kali replied. "I'm starting to trust DeChance. I'm going to feel a whole lot better about all of this if he's right."

She turned before any of them could speak, and sprinted off through the trees again. They followed like dark streaks of lightning, moving so quickly that anyone watching would have seen nothing but smudges against darker shadow as they passed.

They turned when they reached a trail and followed it into the swamp.

It was overgrown and rutted, but wide. A four-wheel-drive vehicle, driven carefully, could still have passed. Kali sped up again, rushing through the brush and overgrown vines, until she burst out into a small clearing, surrounded by moss-laden trees. In the center of that clearing, surrounded by a broken-down cemetery, the ruined frame of an old church stood, gleaming white in the moonlight. There was no sign of a truck—not even tracks where it might have run up to and into the door, which stood open just slightly.

There was no sign of anyone passing in, or out, but there would not be. All of them could cross a lawn without disturbing a blade of grass. How much more adept would such an ancient be? He would not want there to be a trace of his existence if someone stumbled across his resting place. He'd want them to look, and then pass on, seeing nothing.

"He's not here," Kali said. "He is nowhere near. I don't sense him at all. There is nothing."

"We need to move in deeper," Vein said. "According to DeChance's map," he turned slowly and pointed to the northeast, "the land that Starkey owns would be that direction, at an angle, to the far corner."

Kali ignored him and entered the old basement, climbing slowly down the stairs and running her hands over the walls. She circled the interior and kicked at the dirt on the floor. She ran her hands over the damp stone. Bones stuck his head in the door and watched her. Vein waited more patiently, and Bruno moved to the edge of the clearing and paced slowly, watching the trees and shadows among the rest of the ancient graves for any movement.

"What are you doing?" Bones asked.

Kali held up a hand, and continued her search. After a few moments more, she let out a grunt, dropped to the floor of the tomb, and dug at a crack between the slabs of stone making up the floor.

"There!" she said. She pried something loose, and stood, turning and holding her hand out triumphantly.

Bones stepped inside and glanced down. Kali held a small sliver of what seemed to be glass.

"What is it?" he asked.

"It's blood crystal," she said. "Just a tiny shard. He must have planted it here, knowing if I came near he'd sense it. I kept feeling something tugging at me, and then I realized it was my own crystal connecting with something. If we didn't already know that something was strange about this place, I probably never would have noticed it at all."

"So," Vein said from the doorway of the tomb, "he knows we're here."

"Probably has known for a while," Kali said. "We can't stay here, we need to keep moving."

"How long before we get out?" Bones asked, looking a little nervous. "If he catches us right off the bat, then what?"

"Then we trust DeChance," Vein said. "Every time I've ignored the man, he's saved my skin. I'm not a genius, but over time, things can be pounded into my head. I think we'll be okay, but Kali is right, we have to get moving."

They turned, signaled Bruno, who left his vigil and followed, and melted back into the swamp.

"We move around the area," Vein said. "Make it look like we are checking this place from every direction, and then we get the hell out. We just want it to look like we're getting the layout, like we're planning on coming back. I think if we check again, he'll have been by to leave a sign—to make us think he's staying here. We have to be long gone before he's close enough to try exerting control, and I'm thinking he doesn't have to be all that close. We've never met, or dealt with anyone this old or powerful. The rules as we know them are worthless."

"If things go as planned, we should have no trouble," Bones said. "The magic man and his lady are supposed to create a diversion."

"I know," Vein said, "but as much as I trust him, he's never been up against anything quite like this either. Best if we watch out for ourselves, and hope he does the same."

"Someone's coming," Bruno said.

They froze and listened. Kali checked her bloodstone.

"It's not him," she said. "Not unless…"

"Go!" Vein hissed.

The three of them shot off through the trees. They didn't turn to watch for pursuit, they concentrated on speed, following Kali's lead. She didn't take them back toward the plantation house. Instead, she veered toward Old Mill.

They leaped a small stream and broke out onto the edge of a tilled field. Vein held up a hand, and they stopped, all of them turning and stretching their senses.

"Nothing," Vein said. "If he's there…"

"He's shielded," Kali said. "I didn't know it was possible until Donovan told us, but if Starkey is an alchemist…"

"But," Bruno said, obviously uncomfortable breaking in, "he said it would block both ways. If that was Starkey, he didn't know we were there either, right?"

They all turned to look at him, then Vein and Kali exchanged a glance, and they started laughing at the same time.

"Every now and then," Vein said, "you remind me why we keep you around. You're right. So, either that was someone else entirely, or, if it was Starkey, he'll just think we heard him and bolted. Without dropping whatever shield he might use to keep us from sensing him, he can't track us."

"I still think we'd better get out of here," Bones said. "If he figures out how close we were…"

"Yeah, I think we've done what we came to do," Vein said. "We know he was watching for Kali, and we know he knows we're here. Also, if we drew him out, then Donovan should have time for what he needs to accomplish. I just hope the rest of this plan works out. I'd like to see San Valencez again, and I don't like the idea of being some ancient's lap dog."

They flowed out across the field, rushing in on the outskirts of Old Mill. When they reached the trees on the far side of the field, Kali led them along it until it grew wider, and then they crossed. When they came through to the other side, they stepped into another graveyard. This wasn't as old as the one where the tomb in the swamp rested, and it was only slightly better kept. The designs of the tombstones and grave markers showed a span of more than a century of death.

Kali slowed her steps as they neared the center of the graves.

"It was here, wasn't it?" Vein asked, slipping up behind her and wrapping his arms around her.

She nodded. "He died there."

She pointed to a spot on the ground between two small monuments.

"I remember," Vein said. "I saw it…I felt it. We know."

She leaned back into him then. The impact of the sharing hadn't hit her fully until that moment. She didn't need to worry whether they understood; they knew. They hated Starkey just as she did, and their hatred was part of her now. It was strongest with Vein, but they'd all shared it."

"We should go," Bruno said, glancing around. "He may know you'd come here."

"We can't go through town," Bones said. "If anyone saw you…"

"I should be a lot older now. It would have to be someone thinking they saw a ghost, but I know," Kali replied. "We'll go out past the bed and breakfast, back to 17, and then back to the plantation house."

"I hope we still have wine," Bones said. "It's been a long time since I needed a drink worse than now."

"We can stop on the way," Kali said. "One of you will have to go in."

"I'll do it," Bones said. "My treat."

Kali led them out of the graveyard, and the shared memory, and around back of the bed and breakfast. She barely glanced up as she passed, but she wished, just for a moment, that she was back there, turning down sheets and cleaning sinks, looking forward to a hot dinner and her warm bed.

That made her think of her mother, and her father, and her brother, and the anger returned. By the time they hit 17, Vein had to slow her down.

"Someone will see us," he said. "It's okay if they see a group of people walking, but if you are moving like some kind of superhero, someone is going to take notice."

Kali nodded, but it was obvious she wanted to run, to fly, to do anything she could to vent the rage building up inside. Bones made his stop quick, and they slipped out of town quietly. The moon had begun its descent toward morning by the time they turned down the winding overgrown lane toward the Pope Plantation.

When they entered, they were only met by Cleo, who stared up at them with glowing, too-intelligent eyes. Vein started to speak to her, thought better of it, and just nodded. Cleo let out a soft meow, then leaped to the window sill and stared out at the trees and the swamp beyond. The others settled in behind her, opening the wine and spiking it from the blood supply they'd stored in the cellar.

"Come on magic man," Vein said softly. "Let's end this."

CHAPTER TWENTY-SEVEN

"I wish we could use the bloodstone," Amethyst said. She held a smoky crystal in one hand and dug quickly with the fingers of her other hand. She planted the crystal, and moved on.

Across an open, grassy clearing from her, Donovan worked around toward her. They moved in a circle, stopping now and then to plant another stone. When they were done, Donovan stood in the center of the clearing, closed his eyes, and chanted softly. Amethyst stood beyond the makeshift circle and stood watch. She used only the most tentative of spells, knowing that, should Starkey come on them now, they'd have only a moment's notice to defend themselves. If he discovered them before Donovan was finished, or even before the plan was in motion, it was over.

Donovan turned slowly, addressed the spots where each of the crystals had been placed, and then, his arms outstretched, palms down, he spoke a last incantation. When he was done, he hurried to where Amethyst stood.

"It's finished," he said, "and I've cloaked it as well as I can. There is no reason for him to expect such a trap. In fact, he stepped out of the world so long ago that it's possible that ritual magic of the sort I've used was not yet in practice. He may have figured out something similar on his own, but his rituals will be of his own design, and recognizing mine may prove too unfamiliar."

They turned and headed back the way they'd come. The trail was very narrow, and it had not been used in decades, possibly longer. There had once been a road, but now it was difficult going, but they kept a quick pace. Asmodeus glided overhead, just below the branches of the trees trying to stretch over and down and cover the trail.

They startled a deer after about a quarter of a mile, and once they saw what Donovan was nearly certain was a bear lumbering through the trees.

They were both cloaked by enchantments to enhance speed and silence. The residue of the magic might linger, but Donovan thought it was worth the risk if it got them out of the swamp sooner.

"I hope they're okay," Amethyst said.

"Vein can be hotheaded," Donovan said, "but he's not stupid. With any luck, they are already back at the plantation house waiting on us. They may not need rest, but we do, particularly if we're going to pull this off tomorrow. The spell is not a simple one, and there are aspects this time that have never been tested. Besides, as weird as it is to say it, I'm pretty sure if Kali was in trouble, we'd sense it."

Amethyst thought about that a moment, and then nodded. "Maybe we can write it all down when we're done," she teased. "Then we could share a shelf in your library."

"We get out of this one, pretty lady, and we're sharing more than that. I think we'll stick around the area, take a vacation, talk to some people. Then there's the business of featherface up there," he pointed to where Asmodeus slipped beneath the branches, "and his language gap to consider. This has been one strange trip so far. I'd like to think there's some normalcy at the end, such as it is in our lives."

They broke out of the trees, and ahead, the sound of running water called to them. When they reached the bank, Donovan helped her into the rowboat they'd left tied off on the shore, and they cast off. It was a narrow channel, very deep, and moving lazily. The Intercoastal Waterway stretched from Florida up through Virginia, and despite its age, was still an open path along most of the eastern coastline of the United States. George Washington had been among the surveyors involved in its construction, and more history lined the banks than any other stretch of water in the country.

They slipped across unseen, tied the boat off once more, and covered it in branches. It was tucked into a small indentation under the edge of the bank. When they'd done their best to hide it, Donovan pulled a small pouch from one of the many pockets in his coat and untied it carefully. He took a pinch of dust from inside, turned and flicked it out over the top of the small craft.

"Obscura," he whispered.

The branches seemed to bend and twist around the boat, tucking it in even tighter against the bank. Shadows slid over it, and a moment later, it was difficult, even standing a foot away from the water, to tell that anything was there.

"I think it will be safe," Donovan said, tucking the powder away. "We'd better get going."

Now that they were on the far side from the swamp, they were faced only by a small stand of trees. They passed through that and broke out onto a paved trail, running along the waterway. Beyond all of it, across a ditch, Highway 17 stretched north to Virginia and south toward Elizabeth City and Old Mill.

Donovan turned toward Virginia, and they walked quickly along the bank of the waterway.

"This is the border between the states," he said. "The 'Halfway House' stood here, long ago. The laws in the two states were different, as were the jurisdictions of their lawmen. A lot of strange things happened here. Edgar Allen Poe was one guest…he wrote a poem that should be near and dear to Asmodeus' heart near this spot."

"'The Raven'?" Amethyst asked, glancing around with a bit more interest. "Here?"

"Legend has it," Donovan said with a smile, "and I can confirm it, but that is a tale for another day."

They climbed down into a small depression. Stone and brick jutted from the soil on either side.

"This is where we came out a while ago. It used to lead into the wine cellar of the Halfway House. There's nothing left of the place…but this. Perfect for a portal."

With some difficulty, he managed the tricky entrance steps, despite the fact that entropy had long removed the actual stairs. The portal shimmered and opened, and they stepped through. Asmodeus didn't follow. He cried loudly, wheeled, and spun off to soar over the trees, heading cross-country back to the Pope Plantation.

"Can't say that I blame him," Donovan said. "It's a beautiful night to fly."

As they hurried along the corridor, they removed the talismans that blocked their blood bond to Kali and Vein. They felt the tug instantly.

"They're okay," Donovan said, relieved. "Let's get back and finalize our plans, then I'll be ready for bed."

"Maybe," Amethyst said with a soft laugh, "I'll even let you sleep."

CHAPTER TWENTY-EIGHT

George Starkey broke through the trees and stood outside the hatch leading down to his lab. He neither smiled, nor frowned. His expression gave away no emotion, because it had been a very long time since anything as trivial as emotion had marred his concentration.

His work sat untouched, for the moment. He'd sensed the girl's presence. He'd made his way through the swamp to his trap in time to detect others. One other shared the blood bond. She was a smart girl. She'd found his blood crystal, and that meant that she knew he was probably watching for her. He hoped this meant she'd not brought all her allies on that first visit. He needed more. He needed enough others that some could provide food, and others could be his eyes and ears in the world. He needed to re-inject life into his existence before the lethargy of the undead began eating away at his resolve.

He had believed that cloaking himself from the blood bond would give him enough of an edge to move in on them. Somehow, he'd spooked them, but it was fine. The extra challenge actually amused him, and in any case, he hoped that there were more. Four might be enough. If the other two could be caught, and bound, they might do.

Now, with the rising sun scant minutes away, he stood and stretched out his senses to the swamp. He knew there were other powers in those trees and pools, and he respected them. Some were older than he, others much younger. They kept to their boundaries.

This night, however, something had shifted. He didn't know exactly what it was, but he felt a niggling change in his surroundings that he could not quite latch onto. Had someone else entered the game? Was the girl even wiser than he gave her credit for? What would be the danger, if this was true, and could she bring anyone in that was an actual danger, or would she only, in the end, become a greater prize than he'd expected.

He couldn't pinpoint the source of the anomaly, so he turned his attention to the sky. He had not seen the sunrise in three centuries, but he had been so close. He had walked the tree line of the swamp with the rose-tinted daylight climbing slowly over the horizon. He'd felt the first searing heat of more days than he could count. Each time, he waited longer. Each night, he ventured out earlier.

Now, with the dawn encroaching and this next phase of his plan so close to completion, he felt the urge to press his luck. He spun the handle on the hatch and flipped it open, but he did not descend. Instead, he turned, held out his arms, and closed his eyes.

Every fiber of his being shrieked that he needed to be underground, under shade, out of harm's way, but he ignored all of it. He stilled his thoughts, and very softly, he spoke the wards he'd learned so long ago. He turned to the cardinal points, breathing the angelic names and ignoring the burn that had begun itching at his skin. He spoke the last ward, and, just for an instant, the pain lessened. He turned instinctively to the east. Heat shimmered over the surface of his skin. He felt it, and willed it away. He visualized a thin second skin of energy, blocking the deadly rays and sealing him in. He held his ground.

There was pain, but he was used to pain. If it was only the pain, he'd endure it every day to walk in the light and continue his work among the living. He tried to open his eyes. He cracked his lids just a slit, just enough that the light glowing through the opaque skin found its way in.

And he screamed. The searing, burning pain shot through him in that instant as if he'd been dipped in molten lead. He staggered, turned, and dove for the opening behind him. The wards crumbled, and his protection withered to a wisp of smoke, rolling off his burning, smoldering skin. He fell headlong, unable to use the ladder, or to catch himself and stop his fall. He hit hard, managing only to twist slightly and crash onto the floor below with his shoulder.

Bones separated. He screamed again, and rolled to the center of the room where there was no chance of a stray sunbeam finding its way to him. Starkey curled into a ball and rolled back and forth slowly. His mind would not return to him, and that frightened him more than the burning, or the smoke. He'd been a fool, caught up in the moment, and now, in the scant moments of lucid thought afforded him, he was uncertain if he'd ever recover.

But he did. The pain dulled. The burning slowed, stopped, and began to heal. Still, he didn't move. It would be many hours before he was fully healed, and the more energy he expended, the less complete his recovery would be. He needed his strength, and his wits. He needed to lure the girl and her companions to him and then he would feed, and grow stronger.

Instead of rising to go about his work, as usual, George Starkey stayed on the cold stone floor of the central laboratory and thought about the sun. He thought about how close he'd been. He thought about the tingle of those rays over his skin while his eyes were closed. For the millionth time he wondered if it was all in his mind, a trick of ritual and belief. He'd been in that same sunlight seconds before the burning began. The only difference was the opening of his eyes. Could it matter that much? Was it true? Was this the root of the saying that the eyes are the windows to the soul? If so…could he use that? Could he develop other senses to the point he could remain in the dark and walk in the light? Would that be enough?

His mind whirled and gradually stilled. He realized he had been working on the problem a very long time, worrying every angle of it in search of answers. The pain had left him, and his thoughts, while far from still, were his own. Slowly, he rose. He steered clear of the open hatch, retreating into the West Laboratory to prepare for the evening, and the night to come. He didn't want to be careless twice in the same century, and he was still shaken by his earlier lapse in control, and reason.

"Everything must be perfect," he muttered.

He fingered the bloodstone hanging about his chest, and smiled. He'd sprinkled shards of the crystal around the swamp, covering all angles of approach. He would know when they were coming. They would know him, as well, but since they were coming for him, that was of no consequence. They would come, he would take them, and the next phase of his work would get underway in earnest. This time there would be no cloaking his presence. He would be ready.

As much as he yearned to stand and watch the sun rise, in that moment, it felt to George Starkey as if the glowing, fiery ball would never set. He was unused to impatience. It made him feel vulnerable and weak. It was not a sensation conducive to science. It would not do.

Beyond the lab, high in the sky, the sun continued its slow transit, unaware of, or unconcerned by Starkey's discomfort. It was late afternoon, and there were still hours of daylight to come.

Fuming and pacing back and forth across his laboratory, Starkey had forgotten the strange sensation that something had shifted in his realm. He thought only of sunlight, and blood, and he thought if he did not get one or the other very soon, he might, after all the years of his existence, go mad.

CHAPTER TWENTY-NINE

They gathered in the yard out back of the plantation house beneath a large oak tree. The sun had dropped behind the horizon, and the moon, not quite full any longer, but still bright, was rising. They were silent and attentive as Donovan gathered them in a tight circle.

"This is going to be one of the strangest things I've ever tried to pull off," he said. "It's going to take some luck, and a lot of courage. If anyone here is even slightly uncertain about this, speak up now. We all have important parts to play in tonight's—activities. If anyone falters, we could all be in serious danger."

No one moved. He scanned their faces and saw no anger, just intent concentration.

"Okay then. We will be split into two groups. One group will be open to the blood bond. That is where the real danger is. We just don't know how powerful he is. I'll do what I can to protect us, but he's very old, and, for all my knowledge of the occult, I don't know what he's learned, figured out, or changed about what he already knew in three hundred years. His works have not been available for study. He may have tricks up his sleeve that no one has ever seen.

"He knows there are four—two bonded, and two not. I believe that he will assume all four to be vampires, and will also believe he is strong enough to compel any who get near enough. We have to keep him focused, so that group will have to go in bold, confident, and loud. We want to attract him and draw him out. The key is the timing. We can't go now, we have to wait until most of the night has passed. The key is in perception, and the timing has to be perfect. We will start at around two in the morning. We'll take the portal to the Halfway House, and once there, we'll split up."

"Won't he think it's odd, us waiting so late?" Bones asked. "If it were just us, we'd barge in there as soon as it was dark. We'd probably die, sure, but that's how we originally planned it," he turned to the others for confirmation.

"He's right," Kali said. "It's going to feel strange."

"We are counting on that," Donovan said. "He's expecting you to all rush in, try to kill him. He probably thinks you figured out that the blood bond would be too strong, and he might prevent you, so you brought two companions who are not bonded. It's a reasonable plan that, if he was not so old and powerful, might actually work. His mind doesn't work like yours, or mine, though. As dark and devious as he is, he has not interacted with other minds for a very long time. It's likely that anything that varies from his plan is going to throw him off a little. He'll adjust, and he'll understand that things have changed, but he won't follow the logic in the same way someone might who had lived in the world all those years. He'll react in accordance with his own experience, and his own intellect. He will adjust but that adjustment will not allow for the possibility of being surprised or defeated."

"But the sunrise," Vein said. "We'll be as close to it as he will."

"Exactly," Donovan said. "If we want him to believe that you might have discovered something that he has not, we have to make it seem as if the sunrise is not the threat to you that it should be. I know it's a danger, and I have something for that too. "There is also his laboratory. It shouldn't be difficult to find, and we can get you down there for the night if we need to, once we have managed to take him out of the picture."

Vein nodded. "That makes sense. I'd say, we're going to end up there one way or the other."

They laughed nervously.

"If we're careful, we'll be fine," Donovan said. "If things go wrong, you get out of the way. I may not be able to destroy him, but I can hurt him enough to get us out of there. If that happens, though, it's over. He'll never let us near a second time if he believes there is a real threat."

"So, how do I do it?" Kali asked. She stood very still, and she appeared calm, but the tension in the air was so sudden and taut that no one made a sound, until Donovan replied.

"With this," he said.

He stepped over to the tree, reached into a shadowed space between two massive, curling roots, and drew out something long and thin. None of them had spotted it, and he smiled as he turned.

It was a wooden spear, carved to a wicked point at one end. That tip was capped in silver. Brass, copper, silver and gold wire threads wound around the shaft and up over the bottom edge of the silver cap, binding it in place.

"It's dogwood," he said. "There are a lot of different myths about your people," he continued. "You've both heard most of them. You probably also know that it's not an exact science. A Jewish vampire, for instance, would not be threatened by a cross. Silver always works, at least as far as what I've read. Other symbols, spells, incantations and prayers only affect vampires who believed in their efficacy while alive. Neither you, nor Starkey will be much affected by simple Christian symbolism—that's obvious from the way he took you immediately to the basement of a ruined church.

"We don't know a lot about him, but we know the beliefs of his time. This is bound together using certain elements—elements with alchemical meanings and uses. The Dogwood represents the church. He would have rebelled against the organized Catholic Church, having taken off on his own quest for immortality, but that doesn't mean the symbols won't work. He may fear them. It may be a hidden trigger. It's worth a shot, anyway."

"What about that?" Bruno asked, pointing down the haft toward the handle.

There were designs carved into the wood. There was a ring of characters. Below that, about six inches down, was a second ring. In the center, a red cross had been painted onto the haft. Along the length of the wood, the words "Ring a ring o'roses, A pocketful of posies, Atishoo! Atishoo! We all fall down" had been etched carefully.

"It's a nursery rhyme," Donovan said, grinning. "The cross is a plague cross, what they'd have painted on a plague victim's home back in London, at the time Starkey nearly died and lost everything. The rhyme is something children sang, sort of a macabre incantation to death. If there has been any point in Starkey's long existence when true death nearly claimed him, it was the plague-ridden streets of London. That memory—the sight and sense of these symbols—may shake him. Remember, I'm winging it here. He's a wild card, and when you deal with a situation like this, it's better to use a shotgun than a rifle, as they'd say around these parts."

They passed the spear around the group so that everyone could get a good look at it. When it came, at last, to Kali, she held it tightly, staring at the symbols, and the silver cap. When she finally glanced up, she met Donovan's gaze fiercely.

"Thank you," she said.

"It's my pleasure," Donovan said. "If I'd had time, I could have made something more powerful. I brought the materials for this with me from San Valencez, and I spent the last few hours before sunset finishing it."

"No," Kali said. She shook her head violently, and suddenly she had all their attention. "I don't mean the spear. All this talk, all this time, you have planned how we could get close enough to destroy him. You've talked about it as if it was *we* but all along, you knew. You remembered. It's me. I am the one who has to do this. If one of you kills him…none of it matters. It would have been with me forever."

"It's always been yours to do," Donovan said. "I understand that, as do the others. We have to find a way to make it possible, to give you the shot. You will have to take it. It's as simple as that, in the end."

"We'll have your back," Bones said. "Count on that."

Kali turned then, to Vein. She held out the spear, and he placed his hands on it, between hers.

"If something happens to me," she said, "you have to finish this. It has to end tonight. *He* has to end. Promise me."

Vein nodded. "If doing this means none of us walks out of that swamp, that's how it is. For you."

Kali gazed up at him, then slid her hands down the spear shaft to cover his. She drew him close and went up on her toes to kiss him. They all shared the moment. As intimate as it was, none turned aside. Donovan felt the tug of the blood bond tighten and glow, and wondered if, across the fields and swamp and miles, Starkey felt it too. If so, he wondered if it brought a chill, or a thrill, to that ancient heart.

"Okay," Donovan said. "It's a little early to start…"

"A drink," Amethyst suggested. "One glass of wine for the road."

"That," Bones said, "is the best idea I've heard all night."

They all gathered on the old porch. Bruno brought out two bottles of dark red wine, one spiked with blood, and one for Donovan and Amethyst to share. They sat and stood and lounged on the porch of the ancient manor house, staring off into the swamp. The moon had dipped toward dawn, and they drank a toast to her beauty.

Then, at last, Donovan rose.

"It's time," he said. "If you've never traveled through the portals, stay very close, and pay attention. If anyone gets lost in there, they may not find their way back out. At least, not anywhere they want to be."

They disappeared into the shadows. Cleo trotted at Donovan's feet, and Asmodeus, again, chose the high road, banking toward the silver face of the moon and letting out a long, raucous cry. It echoed across the silent fields as he soared off across the trees and disappeared.

CHAPTER THIRTY

Starkey stood still as stone outside his lab. His thoughts were still, and his mind stretched out over the swamp, searching, watching, and waiting for it to begin. He was good at waiting. Time was no longer relevant to him, had not been in a very long time, but with a goal in sight, his patience faltered. There should have been a sign. There should have been movement, the sense of the blood approaching. There was nothing, and still, he waited.

The moon had long since begun her descent. The sun neared, and he dared not think of that so soon after his nearly disastrous folly of the day past. He did not know if he could work, if she waited. If she didn't come and end the anticipation, he would wonder why. He would wonder where she had gone, and why she had not tried to kill him. He would begin to doubt. None of that was acceptable, and so he waited.

Then it happened. He felt a tickle first, and then, a sharp tug, as the girl and her companions passed over a shard of the bloodstone. He opened his eyes, and turned. They had found one of the older ways—from the water. He had not traveled that trail in over a hundred years, and even then it had mostly been his servants. There had been supplies delivered by water at one time, and he'd used that trail to bring them in. After each use, he'd closed it off quickly, like all the other entrances to his land. He didn't want to attract attention. As long as no one began wondering why all the books, strange equipment, parts and pieces of machinery, and other oddities rolled into The Great Dismal Swamp and were never seen again, he was safe, so he varied the points of delivery as widely and often as was possible.

He smiled. This was better than he'd expected. The entrance they'd chosen was more isolated. Even though the night was failing, he was fast, and there would be no one to witness what was to come. He would make short work of these children, drag them back to his laboratory, and be done with it without making even a ripple in the world of the living. It was perfect.

He intended these to return to that world from time to time. He did not want them seen before he was ready, or linked to him in any way that others could discern, though they would be linked to him for the rest of their existence…and the length of that existence would be determined by their own strength of will. To Starkey, it was inconsequential. It was unlikely he'd find anyone in the group intelligent enough to hold meaningful discourse—at least not on his level. It didn't matter because he wasn't looking for companions, only servants.

He strode into the trees, moving slowly at first, but picking up speed as he went. He stretched out his pace, feeling the freedom of the night, and the fresh air. He caught the scent of blood and the tug of the bloodstone on the pendant he wore dragged at him with increasing strength. Within moments he was moving so quickly he nearly flew, and could probably have done so had he kicked off with sufficient force. He slipped through clusters of trees, dodged roots and sailed over cypress tree clumps and patches of water. Once he crossed such a patch so rapidly his feet tapped only lightly on the surface of the water, and he crossed without sinking. If he could have risked the sound he would have laughed. He wondered what Brother Sanchez, who he'd known as a boy, would say if he could see through long dead eyes.

"Madre de Dios," he thought. "It is a miracle."

The four companions made their way directly up the path leading into the swamp from the waterway. They made no attempt to hide their presence, but they hurried their pace. They needed to be in place, in the *right* place, when Starkey found them. Kali had clutched her bloodstone and cried out only moments before, and they knew the ancient vampire was on the move. He was coming for them, and if the increased pressure on the stone was any indication, he was coming fast.

"He's worried about the time," Bones said. "He's afraid he'll get here too late and burn up in the sun before he gets back to safety."

"Or," Vein said, "he's already figured out the sunlight problem to a greater degree than we believe, and he'll just walk in to watch and see if *we* catch fire at sunup."

"There's that," Bones agreed.

They reached the opening in the trees on the border of the nearly round clearing just as Starkey, slowing his headlong rush through the swamp, reached the far side. They stepped into the clearing, walked straight to the center, and stopped.

He was one of the strangest creatures any of them had ever seen. He was tall, thin to the point of defining cadaverous. His clothing hung on him like forgotten rags, and was at least a century and a half out of date. It was, in fact, almost like an afterthought. His hair was silver, and his skin, just as it had been in Kali's shared memory, was a pearl white, like alabaster. If there was blood running through his veins, it was well hidden, and no more than a trickle.

It was his eyes that caught them. They were dark and piercing, filled with energy and intensity, taking them in so fully it was like being stripped and searched, though he was not close enough to touch.

"You know why we're here," Kali said, taking a half step forward and squaring her shoulders. "Come out of the shadows and face me."

He did so, but slowly. He wasn't in a hurry. As he entered the clearing, he hesitated. He cocked his head slightly, possibly sensing something odd, or possibly just sizing them up. Kali took another half step forward.

"What are you waiting for, old man? You aren't scared of a girl? Or maybe it's these"—she waved her hands to indicate Vein, Bones, and Bruno, who stood beside and slightly behind her—"warriors? Your time is up."

Starkey smiled then, and strode into the clearing. He brought his shoulders up, and his entire aspect changed from that of a strange, thin apparition to an imposing, powerful creature of the night in the span of a second.

"You are late," he said. "You tarried, and I cannot abide that. Why did you not come for me the first time? Perhaps it is not I who is frightened."

In that instant, a number of things happened at once. Bruno and Bones lunged, slipping around Kali and Vein to grip Starkey's arms. He seemed more amused by the attack than threatened, but at the same time, a commanding voice called out several words in an ancient language, and the clearing shifted. A wall of silver flame rose on all sides of them, sparking from one buried crystal to the next and closing the ring. Beyond the circle, Donovan strode from corner to corner, setting the wards.

"What is this?" Starkey hissed. He tossed Vein and Kali aside like twigs and turned. He rushed at the circle walling them in. When he made contact with the flames, he screamed. It was as though a train had crashed into a reinforced solid steel wall. There was a slight bowing of the surface, and then he was cast back. He dropped to the ground, stunned, and lay there for a long moment. Then, just as Kali rushed toward him, Starkey remembered he was not alone in the circle. He whirled and rose in a single motion, dancing away from her. There was no hint of humor in his expression now, only cold, calculated fury.

"You dare," he said. "You dare even to try. With this?"

He turned in a slow circle, as if measuring the circle's strength. Kali didn't allow him the moment to contemplate she drove at him, hands raised, and smashed him forward, trying to drive him into the circle again. He turned with a casual shrug, his hand snaked out, and he had her by the throat, lifting her and dangling her above the ground.

"No!" Vein cried. He dove at Starkey, shifted at the last second, and dropped, sweeping his leg at the ancient's knees. Starkey growled, pivoted, and in that instant, Bruno, moving more quickly than any of them would have believed, snatched Kali from him and drew her back. Vein rolled away in the opposite direction, and Starkey faced them once again.

"Clever," he said. "I don't know who he is, but your friend has power. I've not seen such a circle before, though I have known others. I wonder how much things have changed…"

He reached out then with one hand and drew a symbol in the air. Where his finger passed, the symbol remained, burning golden in the darkness. When he was finished, he turned his hand palm up beneath it, and blew into it. The letter floated lazily toward the outer circle. As it neared the silvery flame, it sped, until after a couple of seconds it was no more than a flicker of light. It slammed into the circle and spread out, creating a golden pool of energy against the solid wall of silver.

Just for a second, the circle wavered. It seemed to grow threadbare, as if the lines of power weaving it into a single whole had parted, or frayed. Then it shimmered, grew bright, and snapped back into place with a crackle of energy. Starkey was already writing in the air again, but Bruno had had enough. Starkey was focused on his spell, as if he'd forgotten them again, and Bruno took advantage of that moment to slam into him from behind. The ancient seemed frail, but when Bruno hit him full force, even his greater mass was barely able to move his target. It was enough to interrupt the spell, and the energy Starkey had been focusing exploded in his face. Where Bruno had barely moved him, this explosion threw him back, and before he could regain his balance, he struck the circle again. This time he was prepared, but the blast of blinding light still drove him to his knees. While he was there, Vein rushed in and drove his boot to Starkey's chin. It snapped the old vampire's head back, but seemed to cause no real harm. As he rose, Starkey looked more bewildered by his failure to break the circle than injured by this last jolt.

"Who is he?" he asked, turning.

"Your worst nightmare," Vein said. "A guy with the power to keep you in a circle until the sun comes up."

Starkey stopped, turned toward the tree line in the east, and frowned. There was only the faintest of glows from the sunrise. There was plenty of time to get to safety. He turned back.

"You are trapped, just as I am trapped. If he is your ally, he won't let you burn."

"I'd tell you it's a 'cage match to the death,' but I don't think they had professional wrestling back in the day," Bones said. "We're going to end you."

Starkey smiled again.

"I hardly think so," he said. His hand moved so quickly it was no more than a blur. He drew in the air once more, flicked his fingers toward Bones, and the younger vamp flew back through the air into the circle, striking hard and sliding down to the ground. He didn't move.

"Now," Starkey said, turning back to the group. Then, he stopped. He turned back to where Bones had dropped, only the figure slowly rising to his feet was not the same as he'd attacked moments before.

"What new trick…"

Where Bones had fallen, Vein rose, shaking his head from side to side as if straightening his spine.

"Christ," he said. "That hurt."

Starkey backed away a step. He stared at Vein, and then, turning his head to where Vein had stood before. The original Vein, the one who had not slammed into the wall, walked slowly toward him. They locked eyes, and in that instant Starkey backed up so hard and fast he hit the inside of the circle again and screamed.

Vein waved his hand, and shimmered, and Donovan stood, dead center in the circle, staring at Starkey. Vein joined him, standing shoulder to shoulder, and from behind, Kali stepped forward, shimmered, and became Amethyst. Bruno scowled, broke up in the dim moonlight for just a moment, and then he was Bones, standing and grinning out of the center circle.

"What madness is this?" Starkey demanded. "Who are you? Where is the girl? I sense her blood. I sense it in—*you*—he pointed at Donovan, and then Vein, and then Amethyst. "But...you live?"

Donovan didn't answer. He spoke three words very softly and cast his hand downward. A second circle, in the middle of the one they'd shared with Starkey, blazed to life. It stretched around the four of them, and Starkey let out a howl of rage. On the horizon, the first glow of the coming dawn shimmered in the sky. Starkey slammed into the outer circle again, and again, and then he stopped. From the safety of the inner circle, Donovan and the others watched.

"What happens when that sun rises?" Vein asked. "This doesn't seem the safest place in the world..."

"I will shield you," Donovan said. "Trust me."

"Can he get out?" Amethyst asked. "He rocked the circle before...how much of that can it take?"

"The circle can't be broken," Donovan said. "It is designed to hold a demon, and powerful as he is, Starkey is no demon. It will hold, as long as the circle remains inviolate."

"Kali is shielded?" Vein asked.

Donovan nodded. "She is safe. When the sun rises high enough, and Starkey weakens, she'll have her shot."

Starkey turned then and stared straight at Donovan. He cocked his head to the side, glanced down at the circle, and then, he smiled.

"Inviolate," he said. "Thank you."

Donovan realized his mistake in that instant. Starkey raised his hands, closed his eyes and stood very still.

"Damn it," Donovan said.

"What?" Amethyst said. "What is he...?"

The question became moot. Something skittered along the outside of the circle, a shadow, very low to the ground and moving very quickly. Then another, and another, some larger, some smaller.

"What the hell is that?" Bones asked. "What are those?"

"Animals," Donovan said. "Rats, moles, rabbits, probably others. He's calling to them. He's calling them to disrupt the circle. All he needs is to dislodge the earth around one stone. He can't touch them from here, but..."

At that moment, there was a blinding flash of light. The outer circle split and shattered. Starkey laughed. It was loud and wild, crazed. He turned to them, his grin feral.

"I will make it back," he said. "I will live to work again. I will find you. Now I know you, and I will destroy you."

"Do something," Vein said, bunching to leap forward.

"No!" Donovan said. "You can't. Don't break the circle. I might not be able to shield you from the sun in time. We have to remain still."

"Kali!" Vein called. "Be careful, he..."

Starkey turned. The motion was lightning fast and focused. He stopped, staring into the shadows. Donovan felt the sudden strengthening of the blood bond and shivered. Starkey was calling to Kali, bending her to his will. He was going to try and take her, right under their noses, and there was nothing they could do. With only Bruno to help, Kali was no match for the ancient alchemist, and his power was amplified by anger.

Kali stumbled from the trees. She gripped the spear in both hands, gripped it so hard that her knuckles crackled. She fought every step, almost stopped, and then, stumbled forward again with a low moan. Starkey grinned. He held out a hand, beckoning to her.

"Come, girl," he said. "I have work to do; you have distracted me."

"Go to hell," Kali grated. She continued to fight, but the closer she grew to Starkey, the weaker her struggles. She crossed the clearing as slowly as she could. The cloak Donovan had provided her blocked the encroaching dawn, but could do nothing to prevent Starkey's will from seeping into her mind, and her body, taking control and drawing her near.

"Come now," he said. He reached for her hand, and half turned, ready to flee through the rising sun.

Two more forms burst from the shadows. Bruno, no longer cloaked in the illusion that had made him the image of Donovan, dove after Kali, keeping low. He tried for Starkey's legs, but the ancient sidestepped and lashed out with one foot, sending Bruno sprawling. Cleo, who'd followed, sprang at Starkey's face, but he was too fast. She slid through the air, missing him cleanly as he started for the edge of the clearing.

"No!" Vein cried. He dove forward, shot through the circle and broke it with a snap. He dove for Starkey, even as the ancient snatched at Kali's hand and bolted for the trees.

"Damn," Donovan said. He followed Vein, raised his hands, and began a chant that slid a shadow over the clearing. It was nebulous, not perfect, but blocked most of the sunlight.

They were too late. Starkey lurched into the trees, Kali screamed, and they slipped from sight.

"After them!" Vein cried. He shot off after Starkey, Bruno and Bones at his heels, and Donovan, still trying to form the curtain of shadow overhead, followed.

CHAPTER THIRTY-ONE

George Starkey felt more alive than he'd felt in centuries. He gripped the girl by the arm and dragged her along behind him like a bag of grain. She fought him, but it was puppy-weak and pathetic. He didn't even bother to take the spear from her hand. There was no time. He was racing now, pitting his mind, and his will, against the speed of the rising sun.

They were closing in on his laboratory, and if he could get her down that hole, close the hatch, and set his wards, it was over. They would never get in. If he needed to he could stay inside for years, and though it would hurt her, the girl would survive as well. He could break her, send her out again, and start over.

There was one final stand of cypress trees between him and his goal, and he raced toward it, ignoring the girl's wails and the sound of pursuit—too late, and too slow. He didn't know who the mage had been, but he'd find out, and he'd deal with him in his time.

But he didn't make it to the trees. Before he reached them, an old woman stepped from between the bent trunks and waving branches. She stood very still, just clear of the trees, leaning on a wooden staff, and waiting.

Starkey growled. He had no time to deal with the woman, or whatever she represented. He felt the rays of the rising sun searing the skin of his arms and face. He veered to one side and tried to slide around this new threat. The first arrow struck him high on his right shoulder. The impact, though it should have been trivial, actually spun him around.

Before he could react, a second shot caught his collar bone on the opposite side, and he screamed. He released Kali, who dropped away to the side, and reeled back. The arrows burned. He had no idea how, or why it was so, but it was a moment for action. He had eternity to sort the details, but he had to get past this old woman, and whoever else was out there. He feinted to the left, as if shifting directions, and then surged to the right, moving so quickly he seemed to disappear from one point and reappear at another, just inside the stand of trees. He threw back his head and laughed. He was going to make it.

He plunged ahead, but something was wrong. The trees, already dense, closed in before him. He slammed into a trunk that had seconds earlier leaned the opposite direction. Vines and branches slithered like serpents, gripping his ankles. He kicked free and tried to fight his way through, ripping branches away with all of his otherworldly strength, moving as if swimming through a sea of wood and leaves, but it was too much. The grove closed in on him. He was pinned, arms and legs, and turned.

The back of his head burned, and he cried out. He closed his eyes and began to chant. It was his moment. He would overcome the sunlight, or it would end. He had no more time for flight, and no more strength to fight, but he had his mind. He kept his eyes closed and spoke quickly, forming the shield he'd worked so long to perfect, encasing himself in its shimmering glow. He closed his mind to the world and concentrated his will and his essence on one simple thing. Survive. Live. Do. Not. Burn.

Kali rolled to her feet. She glanced up into the sky in panic. The sun had topped the trees, and she was only just aware of it. It didn't burn. Whatever Donovan had done to protect her, the headlong flight in Starkey's grip had not weakened it. She did not feel her usual strength or speed, but neither did she feel pain.

Before her, between where she stood, and the strange, knotted mass of limbs and branches that held Starkey, the old woman stood, watching her. She did not seem nervous, or particularly angry. Her eyes were bright and curious, and though her hair was silver and blew about her face like a wisp of clouds, she was beautiful.

Another figure melted from the trees then. This girl was younger, but in some way so similar to the old woman that it was startling. She carried a bow. There was an arrow knocked and ready. The girl's eyes were clear and intelligent, but wary. She reminded Kali of deer she'd seen, just on the edge of the forest, beautiful, but ready to flee at a moment's notice—and dangerous if cornered.

"Who are you?" Kali asked, turning to the old woman.

"I am Nettie, girl, not that it matters. You've heard of me. Your ma and pa heard of me too, and theirs. I've always been here. When that one," she lifted her staff and pointed back toward the trees, "came to the swamp, I was here. I have waited a long time to catch him out of his gopher hole, and I thank you for your part in it."

Kali stood up straight now. Her eyes blazed, and every ounce of her pain returned to her—every shivering, piano-wire of hatred snapped, and she turned toward the trees.

"He is mine," she said. She didn't ask this, nor did she wait for agreement, or permission. She took off for the trees at a trot, ignoring the strangeness of moving by day, and the stare of the girl with the bow.

"I would not deny you," Nettie said. "You have come too far, and he has taken too much. This will not bring them back…but it is closure. It is the circle come full, Alicia. It is time for this to end."

Kali stopped and turned back, just for a second. She had not heard the name Alicia in a long time. She searched her memory, and found that she did know this woman. More precisely, she knew *of* this woman. Nettie. The swamp witch. The Earth Mother. She recalled tales of festivals, harvest time, and there was something about a bonfire—the light of that fire burning still in the old woman's eyes.

"Not now, girl," Nettie said softly. "You have time to remember. End this."

Kali turned toward the trees, lifted the spear Donovan had given her, and disappeared into the trees.

Just as she dropped out of sight, Vein, Bones, and Bruno, who had been forced to wait for Donovan, stepped into the clearing on the far side. The girl shifted, her arrow still ready. A dark, billowing shadow floated over the group as they came into view. Donovan gave half his attention to maintaining the sun shield, and the other to the old woman facing them.

"*Who* is *that*?" Amethyst asked.

"I don't know," Bones said solemnly, watching the old woman barring their way and leaning on her staff, "but if she says 'You shall not pass!', I'm out of here."

CHAPTER THIRTY-TWO

The trees held Starkey very still. They blocked most of the sunlight, forming a sort of canopy overhead with the ancient trapped in its center. His eyes were closed, and his lips moved, speaking a steady stream of words that Kali did not understand. She approached cautiously.

The spear Donovan had given her was solid, and though she felt almost mortal, shielded as she was from the sunlight by Donovan's spell, she didn't hesitate. Tiny puffs of smoke rose from exposed bits of Starkey's skin, but though in places the sunlight struck him directly, he was not destroyed. Something shimmered along the surface of his body, and Kali realized with a start that he had formed something very similar to what Donovan had given her.

"Be as quick as you can," the mage had said. "It will protect you, but it's like speeding your metabolism. It is fueled by your essence, the force that keeps you moving and living. The effort to walk when you should not be able to walk will cut away at your reserves. If you don't get back under cover, and released from the spell, it will devour you."

Was it the same for Starkey? She couldn't tell. He was still working to form the shield, and she didn't think he was aware of her presence. She took a moment to study him. The figure that had seemed so powerful, so overwhelmingly strong and charismatic now looked only pale and weak. The milky, pearlescent hue of his skin was sickly and lifeless. His clothes hung in ruined rags. His features were sunken and drawn back like the rictus of a skeleton.

He was pinned about two feet off the ground. Bent, twisted cypress trees wrapped him tightly, binding both his legs and his arms, another long root snaked up and around his throat. Kali stepped onto the lower trunk of one of the trees binding Starkey's legs and stood over him. She watched, and she waited, but he showed no signs of ceasing his chant, or opening his eyes. She'd waited long enough.

"You killed my brother," she said softly.

Starkey did not react.

"You killed my mother, and my father."

Still nothing, though there was an almost imperceptible twitch at the corner of one of the ancient's eyes.

"You took my life, and my family. You tried to make me a slave."

There was a crunch of branches and leaves. Kali glanced over her shoulder and saw that Donovan, Vein, Bones, Bruno, and Amethyst had stepped into the trees. Behind them, still standing quietly in the clearing, as if nothing more than an observer, Nettie watched. The younger girl stood at the old woman's shoulder, also watching.

Kali turned back.

"You have lived a very long time," she said. "You have killed and taken and fed your own sick dreams for too long. It ends today."

In her mind, she heard a voice. She'd have sworn it was her father's, but at the same time, it might have been Johndrow, or Donovan. It echoed and twisted through her memories, and dredged up words—the ritual.

"In the name of my father, and my mother," she said. "In the name of my life, which you stole, I will end you. From ash to ash, from fire to fire."

She raised the spear, and in that instant, Starkey's eyes snapped open. He saw her then, saw the stake, and over her shoulder, for a fleeting moment, saw the hint of the sun. He arched, trying to break free of the trees, but they only held him tighter, and as he presented himself, Kali struck.

She drove the stake down hard, slamming the silver tip through his chest and driving it deep. It was good that it was long, because she put all of herself behind the blow. She dredged up her anger and her hatred and she screamed. The wooden shaft burned itself in Starkey's heart, stopping only when her hands reached his flesh. She drew back, reeling and nearly falling.

Vein stepped forward, and as she toppled, he caught her in his arms, though it was obvious he had little strength left to him. They had all been in the sunlight too long. Vein turned toward Donovan.

"We have to get…"

The words died in his throat. There was a sizzling, crackle of fire. The trees, gripping Starkey tightly only moments before, released and dropped his suddenly flaming body to the ground. Vein took a step back, and then another. They all stood, and they watched, as George Starkey, impossibly, rose to his knees. He actually crawled a step toward them as his skin hissed and sizzled, cracking and falling away from the bone. What had been his mouth was open wide, but no sound emerged. Where his eyes had been, pits of fire flickered and burned, searing the inside of his drying, cracking skull.

With a roar, Bruno surged forward. He raised his large, booted foot and drove it down into the haft of the spear. His weight toppled Starkey back and drove the spear into the earth. It broke the carcass into two pieces, and then, seconds later, there was nothing but ash and dust. The flames sucked in on themselves and were simply gone.

The silence was absolute. There was no wind. No insects sang or chirped or buzzed. No leaves brushed against branches, and though several among them were mortal, and needed to, no one breathed.

Then, as if waking from a dream, Donovan sprang into action.

"Quickly," he said. "Starkey was heading this way."

They moved as a single unit. The cloud overhead held, but seemed thinner, and none of the young vampires had much energy to argue. The trees, so dense that Starkey had hit them like a wall, parted before them, and in the clearing ahead, Donovan saw the hatch leading down to the laboratory.

"In there," he said. "Bruno, you first, then Bones. Vein can hand Kali down to you, and follow. Amethyst and I will close the hatch. We'll be back for you after the sun falls. We have loose ends to tie up."

Vein nodded, and Bruno was already climbing over the lip of the hatch and dropping down into the chamber below. The others followed, and when she saw Vein falter, Amethyst rushed over to help him lower Kali through the opening. Vein dropped in after her without bothering to use the ladder and Amethyst dropped the hatch in place, turning the wheel to seal it.

She stepped back and stood beside Donovan who, finally, released the spell he'd held all that time. The shadow dispersed with a whoosh of energy that ended in a soft pop. He turned, started to say something, and then, without a sound, his knees buckled, and he dropped to the soft earth in a heap.

"Donovan!" Amethyst cried.

She ran to his side. He was breathing shallowly, but his face was pale, and when she shook his shoulder, he didn't respond.

"Let me see, child," a voice intruded. It was dry and whispery, old as the wind.

Amethyst glanced up to find Nettie standing over her. Behind her, the young girl stood, her bow planted firmly by her foot, watching intently.

"He's used too much energy," Nettie said. "Damn fool thing to do, protecting vampires, but there you have it. The sun is hungry too—it thirsts. He denied it, and now, he has paid."

"Will he…?"

Nettie laughed then, and the dryness cracked off her voice like ice dropping from the eaves in a spring thaw.

"This one? He is strong, girl. Never forget that. He needs rest. He needs drink and shade."

She turned and made some gesture that Amethyst missed to the girl, who disappeared in a flash of bare legs and long hair. A moment later, there was a crashing sound in the brush, and, to Amethyst's astonishment, a very large deer stepped from the trees. She stood very still, as if afraid of spooking the animal.

"Don't you worry about him," Nettie cackled in delight. "He's here to help. You'll need to help the girl get him on the animal's back. He'll take it from there. He'll get him back to that dark place you've been stayin'. Then he's all yours."

Amethyst wanted to protest. She wanted to say something, anything, that would shift things back into any kind of normalcy, but words failed her. She stood, and when she did, there was a cry from above. They all turned their eyes to the sun, and Asmodeus dropped in on them with a flap of wings and a soft cry. The old bird landed directly on the tip of one of the deer's horns. The animal shook its head, irritated, but the old crow clung tightly, glaring at them balefully.

"Do-no-van," it garbled. Then it settled and the deer, eyes rolling up to try and get a look at the odd creature, settled.

Amethyst laughed then. She laughed so hard she lost her footing. She stumbled, fell back and dropped to the ground, sitting beside Donovan's prone body, tears streaming down as Nettie, the girl, the deer, and the crow, watched her in amusement. It took a long time to control her mirth. The stress and the nerves, the spent energy, all of it bubbled out in that one long burst of laughter.

Finally, she managed to get back to her feet, and with some effort, she and the girl lifted Donovan across the back of the stag, resting his head between the antlers, beneath Asmodeus' haughty stoic gaze. Slowly, they started off through the swamp. The girl led the deer; Nettie and Amethyst walked beside, helping to keep Donovan in place.

Behind them, the sun beat down on the hatch leading to George Starkey's laboratory, relentless, but helpless to penetrate its secrets. It was after noon before the group reached the trees lining the fields of the abandoned Pope Plantation. By then, Donovan had lifted his head weakly, taken in his situation, and groaned.

He slid from the deer's back, leaned on the animal a second, and whispered in its ear. It shook its head, turned to him, and Amethyst would later swear the creature nodded gravely before trotting away into the trees. The girl was gone, as well, and only Nettie stood beside them in the overgrown field.

"You have done me a service," she said, turning to Donovan. "I don't forget. When you need something, next time, you don't have to bring the whiskey."

Donovan was shaky, still, but upright, and he managed a smile. "And miss the pleasure of sharing a drink?" he said. "You saved us back there."

"You were fine," Nettie said. "Saved the young dead one, maybe, and her friend. Thing is, I've been trying to dig that dark one out for a long time. When he's weak, he's sealed away, and he's done harm to the swamp over the years. No respect for the wildlife, or for the people. Nothing but a dark, empty hole for a soul and that mind. He was smart..."

"Brilliant," Donovan said. "I hope to drag some of his journals out of that laboratory before I leave. Need to get them packed up and stored safely."

"Going to need a big box," Nettie cackled.

"I have ways of getting it out of there," Donovan said. "Storage might be a problem, but I've managed so far."

"Sure," Amethyst cut in drily. "You could stack them on your bed. Who needs that, when you have books?"

Nettie's laugh, this time, was loud and long. "I believe you will find a way," she said. "Now, ol' Nettie has things to attend to. Things to fix and mend. And I have to see where that girl got off to."

"Thank you," Donovan said.

"And thank you," Nettie replied. "You see Cletus again, you tell him we sent our regards. The girl is well...I believe she has his eyes..."

And then, without another word, the old woman was simply gone. She didn't melt into the ground, or disappear in a theatrical puff of smoke. She was there, and then the wind whistled gently through the trees overhead, and she was gone.

Amethyst tucked herself under Donovan's arm to help support him, and they started across the field toward the plantation.

"I hope there's some of that wine left," Donovan said wearily. "I need a drink, and one long, deep sleep."

Asmodeus dove in ahead of them, making a beeline for the porch, and Cleo, who had followed along quietly, bounded ahead and stopped, sitting on the porch and waiting for them to catch up. As the two of them stumbled up the steps and in through the old, rotting doors, Amethyst smiled. With Cleo rubbing against her leg, and the old crow clutching Donovan's shoulder tightly, it suddenly felt very much like a family.

CHAPTER THIRTY-THREE

The group stood outside near the tracks in Rocky Mount, North Carolina, watching as several wooden crates, the journals, books, and equipment from George Starkey's laboratory, were being loaded onto a freight car. Vein and the others were booked into a special sleeper car, courtesy of Johndrow and the council. Boarding was in ten minutes, and the group was in high spirits.

"Sure you don't want to ride back with us, magic man?" Vein asked. "I have the feeling it's going to be a considerably calmer trip than on the way out here."

"Not this time," Donovan said. He stood with his arm around Amethyst. "We're going to hang around here for a while, take in some sights, and lay low for a while. You'll take care of my cargo for me?"

"Of course," Vein said. "We'll store it at old Joel's bank. It will be there when you get back. Maybe we'll come help you move enough of the crap out of your den to get it inside."

"I'll take you up on that," Donovan laughed. "You'll be surprised at the room I have, though, when I need it."

Vein just shook his head. "I'll believe it when I see it," he said. "Every time I come over, you are moving things off the chairs so I can sit. There are a lot of crates here."

Donovan just smiled.

"It's a system," he insisted. "I know where everything is…"

"Yes," Amethyst nodded gravely. "He knows it's in one of those piles somewhere…"

They all laughed. The conductor opened the door and dropped the steps for passengers to enter. Bruno and Bones picked up their collective bags, which didn't amount to a lot. They'd traveled light, and when they'd contacted Johndrow, he and Vanessa had been so relieved to hear they were alive he'd arranged the return trip himself, sparing no expense. The Council had several special sleeper cars that they owned and maintained. They had to let the railroad know ahead of time to have one in the train, but they'd managed it in record time.

"What are you two going to do way out here in the sticks?" Bones asked. "I can't wait to get back to the city. If I see another cotton field or cypress tree I'll scream. I need a good week at Club Chaos just to *start* to feel normal again."

"I'm going to show Amethyst some sights," Donovan said, "and I believe we'll stop in on a few old friends before we leave. We have to settle up with Cletus Diggs for the use of the plantation house, and I'm hoping to get the full story on that place before we leave. We also promised him a story, and I'm going to have to give him something."

"I should have talked to him," Kali said with a shy smile—one of many new and improved expressions that had been replacing the intense glare and the fierce frown they were all so accustomed to. "I probably look about the same as I did when they ran my picture in the local paper…that would have opened his eyes."

"Cletus has seen some things himself," Donovan said. "I doubt we'd shock him too much, and that might be a bit more of a story than even he is ready for. I'll come up with something. Then there's Bullfinch…we all owe Geoffrey for the information he gave us and for the dust he gave me to deal with our friend back in Memphis. I saved back a few things for him to look over from Starkey's lab. It should be enough to keep him busy for some time to come."

"Don't stay gone too long," Kali said, meeting his gaze. "When you get back…if you don't mind…I'll be having a party of sorts. I'm told it's a tradition, but I would do it anyway. I'd like you to be there, both of you. Bring Cleo and Asmodeus, if you can. I'll make sure Johndrow and Vanessa are there. It's important."

"We will come, of course," Donovan said. "We wouldn't miss it."

"I'll be celebrating my freedom," she said. "I believe that I'd like to share that moment, and more, with the two of you."

Bruno looked almost hurt at this, and Kali turned to him. "You too, you big idiot—both of you. God, what did you think?"

Bruno grinned sheepishly. Impulsively, Kali stepped forward and embraced him. Then she turned and hugged Amethyst as well. Vein stood by quietly, but Bones broke into a big grin.

"I never would have believed it," he said. "Next thing she'll be wearing shirts with sparkly unicorns and rainbows."

Kali spun on him, fast as lightning, and shoved him hard. Bones toppled over in a heap, clattering to the ground in a pile of luggage, as they all burst into bright laughter.

Moments later, the four boarded the train, and Donovan turned to Amethyst. He held out his arm.

"Shall we?" he asked. "They tell me the barbecue here is to die for."

She took his arm, sniffed, and shook her head. "Then I'll be having lobster," she said.

They left the platform as the train's air brakes whooshed and the great wheels began to slowly turn. They'd left Vein's car idling at the curb. Donovan held the door for Amethyst, and then climbed in. Asmodeus sat calmly on the dashboard, and in the rear, Cleo let out an irritated yowl.

"Patience," Donovan said. "A little patience please. We have a long trip ahead, and for once, I'm going to sit back and enjoy the drive."

He pulled out into the old part of Rocky Mount and nosed down Marigold toward Highway 17, and roads north. The moon was high in the sky, and there were no clouds. Amethyst scooted over and laid her head on his shoulder. With an odd, hillbilly blues station jangling out of the radio, they rolled on into the night.

Later, as they neared Old Mill, Donovan spotted a sign alongside the road, and he started to laugh.

World's Largest Cockroach, Ten Miles on Right. Fresh Produce!

"Honey," he said, controlling his mirth, "we are *still* not in Kansas."

"Good," Amethyst said sleepily. "Now find me a drink, and a bed. We have a long day ahead, and something tells me, no matter how hard we might wish, it won't be simple, or relaxing."

"God," Donovan said, "I hope not."

He nosed into the driveway to the old Bed and Breakfast nestled in against The Great Dismal Swamp and drove into the shadows. They had reservations, and he was ready for a long, peaceful sleep.

ABOUT THE AUTHOR

David Niall Wilson has been writing and publishing horror, dark fantasy, and science fiction since the mid-eighties. An ordained minister, once President of the Horror Writers Association and multiple recipient of the Bram Stoker Award, his novels include *Maelstrom*, *The Mote in Andrea's Eye*, *Deep Blue*, the Grails Covenant Trilogy, *Star Trek Voyager: Chrysalis*, *Except You Go Through Shadow*, *This is My Blood*, *Ancient Eyes*, *On the Third Day*, *The Orffyreus Wheel*, The DeChance Chronicles, including *Heart of a Dragon*, *Vintage Soul*, *My Soul to Keep*, *Kali's Tale*, and the stand-alone spinoff *Nevermore—A Novel of Love, Loss & Edgar Allan Poe*. His novels in the O.C.L.T. series include *The Parting*, *Crockatiel*, and the novella *The Temple of Camazotz*. He is also the author of the memoir/cookbook *American Pies: Baking with Dave the Pie Guy*. David can be found at: www.davidniallwilson.com and can be reached by e-mail at david@davidniallwilson.com.

MYSTIQUE
PRESS
CROSSROAD
PRESS

www.ingramcontent.com/pod-product-compliance
Lightning Source LLC
Chambersburg PA
CBHW060608310726
48982CB00008B/1271/J

* 9 7 8 1 9 4 9 9 1 4 3 6 8 *